BATTLE CRY

BATTLE CRY

Chet Cunningham

Thorndike Press • Chivers Press
Waterville, Maine USA • Bath, England

This Large Print edition is published by Thorndike Press, USA
and by Chivers Press, England.

Published in 2001 in the U.S. by arrangement with
Chet Cunningham.

Published in 2001 in the U.K. by arrangement with
the author.

U.S. Hardcover 0-7862-3381-8   (Western Series Edition)
U.K. Hardcover 0-7540-4601-X   (Chivers Large Print)
U.K. Softcover   0-7540-4602-8   (Camden Large Print)

The text of this Large Print edition is unabridged.
Other aspects of the book may vary from the original edition.

Set in 16 pt. Plantin by Rick Gundberg.

Printed in the United States on permanent paper.

British Library Cataloguing in Publication Data available

Library of Congress Cataloging-in-Publication Data

Cunningham, Chet.
  Battle cry / Chet Cunningham.
    p. cm. — (Pony soldiers)
  ISBN 0-7862-3381-8 (lg. print : hc : alk. paper)
    1. Sheridan, Philip Henry, 1831–1888 — Fiction. 2. Indians
of North America — Wars — Fiction. 3. Large type books.
I. Title.
PS3553.U468 B38 2001
813´.54—dc21   2001027649

BATTLE CRY

Chapter One

Black Kettle stared out the flap of his tipi and watched the snow falling slowly like white hair on Mother Earth. He knew he would die before the snow flakes falling now melted into the lush green growth of Spring.

He had experienced a vision from the Great Eagle himself. He had soared down out of the blue sky and then the giant bird lifted Black Kettle high over the Washita so he could see for two days' ride in all directions. Black Kettle had seen his own warriors heading out on a raid into Kansas. He had warned them not to go. He could see the twisting pattern of the Washita River as it wound to the south and west.

The Great Eagle gave a terrible scream of pain and almost dropped Black Kettle as it turned to the north and the chief saw a sea of blue-shirted cavalrymen and foot soldiers. They came in an unending wave a mile wide and stretching to the north into the mists, staining the pure white snow with the terrible blue, bringing death and the end of life to

Cheyenne People as they had always known it.

Black Kettle would die.

The Indian chief could not make out the vision clearly, but there was snow everywhere, deep snow. In places it showed red with Indian blood. Women and children ran screaming into the snow and the thin ice over the river. Warriors rushed from their buffalo robes still sleep-dulled and naked as they tried to fight the terrible attack by the never-ending hordes of Pony Soldiers.

Black Kettle saw himself and his wife on a war pony, but then the mists closed in and he could see nothing else that happened.

Blood spread over half the site where his village had stood, Indian blood. Then the Great Eagle lifted him so high that for a moment Black Kettle thought he was already dead and ascending into the Great Heaven. But at once the vision faded and he sat again before his small warming fire in his tipi, with the snows of November starting to fall outside covering the grass and leaves of fall.

This would be the winter of the death of his Cheyenne band.

Black Kettle rose and went to the tipi flap and looked at the snow. It was only an inch deep so far. Soon it would blow and drift in places as tall as a war pony. No white eye

Pony Soldier troop could drive through that much snow and attack his village. Snow, they must have more snow to close them in, to protect them from the soldiers who would be forced to stay in their wooden tipis at their tiny forts.

Perhaps the vision was for another time — in the spring after the snow melted.

No. He would not live to see the snow falling today melt and nourish Mother Earth in the Spring.

Yellow Dog and Four Fingers stepped into the tipi through the open flap and stood silently, waiting for Black Kettle to recognize them. He did so, nodding at them at once, and they moved around to the left inside the tipi so they would not come between their host and his fire.

Black Kettle waved them to sit down near the fire, and both did so, then watched him closely. Both were greatly honored Cheyenne warriors. Both had fought beside him in many battles and gone on countless raids with him. They were proud Cheyenne fighters.

"Black Kettle, the council is meeting, we want you to come, to speak your mind."

Black Kettle frowned. He had not wanted this kind of a confrontation. He was much more "peace" minded than the young bucks and the older warriors. "You know how I feel.

9

I have told you many times."

"A raiding party is ready to go north to the Kansas place. You will want to talk against it."

Black Kettle nodded, stood and without a warm buffalo robe, walked through cold and the falling snow to the largest tipi in the camp, that of the medicine man, Small Claw. Nearly thirty members of the council stood inside the tipi. It was already full and overflowing.

Black Kettle studied as many of the faces as he could see, then he began:

"We are a warrior tribe. We live by hunting and raiding. Warfare has been our prime purpose in life. But those days are done with, gone forever. The Cheyenne nation must realize this, we must know for certain that the White Eyes and their Pony Soldiers are in our lands to stay. They will take over our hunting grounds and our camp sites. They will measure and divide our land and build railroads and roads and put up fences.

"You have heard this before. You do not heed my warnings. My magic is not as strong as it once was. These raids on the White Eyes will bring only vengeance and destruction down upon us.

"We have word that the Pony Soldiers have pushed south from their fort in Kansas and have set up a new camp on the North Canadian River. They will use this camp to launch attacks against us. We must accept the land and the protection from the Soldier General Hazen down river at Fort Cobb. I will go there soon with whoever wishes to go with me.

"Yes, it will mean a different way of life for the Cheyenne, but we will survive. No longer will we need to raid the White Eyes. We will have food for our bellies and our women and children will be safe from the Pony Soldiers.

"I ask you again, do not go on this raid. Let the White Eyes ranchers alone. We do not need their horses. We have parfleches filled with dry buffalo meat and pemmican. Let us stay within our camp, defend ourselves, and rest and regain our strength for the Spring."

Black Kettle reached for the peace pipe, then looked around the assembly. He sighed and did not light the pipe. Everyone who agreed with him would smoke it, but he saw no support in the eager faces, all waiting to start on the raid.

Yellow Dog stood and looked at Black Kettle.

"The days of the Cheyenne are not over, great and honored Chief, Black Kettle. We are strong! We are proud! We will fight the White Eye and the Pony Soldiers wherever we find them. We should gather all our warriors and strike the soldiers at this camp on the far Canadian river.

"But for now, the snow is starting. It will cover our tracks. We will slash to the north, destroy several ranches, take their horses and return, and the Pony Soldiers will never find us. We are Cheyenne!"

There was no need to pass the peace pipe. Almost to a man the Cheyenne warriors bellowed their approval. They trooped outside and left the medicine man Small Claw, Black Kettle and his long time trusted friend and advisor, Little Robe. They looked at each other.

"The snow is still falling giving Mother Earth her white blanket so she can stay warm in the frigid winter to come," Small Claw said.

"It will cover up the tracks of the warriors going up to the Kansas place, but what about coming back?" Black Kettle asked.

Little Robe was a robust man with many summers. He stared at both the men and shook his head. "We must go tomorrow toward the tipi of this Soldier General you have talked about. We go to this Fort Cobb. I will be at your side and with as many warriors as I can bring."

"We must go into the reserve the White Eyes leaders and their Pony Soldiers have prepared for us," Black Kettle said. "At least we must take our women and children. If not, the future of the Cheyenne is as dark as an angry sky just before a thunderstorm."

They all nodded. Black Kettle looked up sharply. "I will die before this snowfall melts," he said softly to the Medicine Man.

"How. . . ."

Black Kettle lifted his hand to silence the man. "The Great Eagle came and lifted me up high so I could see my own death. The Pony Soldiers will come and find us here on the Washita. We must think about moving downstream to safety."

"At Fort Cobb?" Small Claw asked.

"At Fort Cobb," Black Kettle said. "Yes, we will go tomorrow."

Each of the Cheyenne warriors who rode out into the light snowfall that early November morning in the year 1868 was excited, ready for a daring raid into Kansas and ready to capture many prize horses and win honors and make coups. It had been three months since their last raid and they were eager for the action.

Each warrior rode his second best war pony and trailed his finest animal behind on a tether. It would be hard going through the snow if it got much deeper. Yellow Dog at the head of the band assured them that there would be no more than two hands of snow. It was early in the winter season. But the snow would be plenty to mask their tracks for the journey into Kansas.

Yellow Dog had sent Four Fingers on a scouting excursion a week ago into the Kansas lands and he had found three ranches close together. They were near the Cimarron so the warriors could strike and be away quickly. They would have a long ride, but it would be worth it.

"Plenty of horses," Four Fingers said. "They herd the White Eye buffalo with the long horns and use many horses. We should find over a hundred on the ranches!"

To the Cheyenne the horse was still the measure of a man's wealth. Yellow Dog had nearly forty himself, and would like to capture five or six more on the raid. Thirty warriors rode through the gently falling snow.

Yellow Dog scoffed remembering Black Kettle's prattle. It was what the old men all said when they got too feeble to go on the raids. Bow down to the White Eyes, go where they send us. Let them ruin the Cheyenne way of life. Yellow Dog would have none of it. He would live and hunt and raid where he wished to for as long as he could draw a breath.

True, he knew the raiding would be harder and harder, as the White Eyes became more numerous, and the Pony Soldiers pushed them and chased them after the raids.

But this was winter. A time for renewal and rest — after this and one or two more quick raids, he would be satisfied to settle down and sleep until midday and service each of his three wives every day, and make sure his horses found enough food through the skiffs of snow and ice.

Winter was the traditional time of rest for most of the Plains Indians, Yellow Dog knew. But he wanted these three more raids. The Pony Soldiers would not fight in the winter. The band would be safe there on the Washita far from any Pony Soldier camp.

Even the new place the soldiers used on the far Canadian did not bother him. The Cheyenne were safe. They would rest and prepare for war in the summer. The warm weather was time for war. Then their ponies would be filled and fat from the spring grass, and over their thinness and short stamina from the sparse winter feed.

Summer was the time for raiding and war. Winter was time for rest and recuperation. It would ever be so.

Even the White Eyes followed the Indian's way of fighting.

The line of Indian horsemen followed the course of the Washita River upstream, then when they were west of the Antelope Hills, they turned north and struck out for Kansas through what some of the White Eyes were calling Texas. They would cross the North Canadian and then when they hit the Cimarron they would follow it upstream to the ranches.

More than a hundred horses ready for the taking! Yellow Dog smiled just thinking how easy it would be.

The snowfall picked up in intensity now and it clung to horse and rider. Soon the warriors, snugly warm in their finest buffalo robes, were so white they looked like wandering snowmen mounted on war ponies that also soon took on a layer of wet snow.

The temperature dropped lower and the wet snow froze where it hit.

Yellow Dog knew they had a long ride, two hard days. It might take them three in the snow if it got much deeper. Still, Small Claw, their medicine man, had guaranteed that there would be no more than knee deep snow during this storm. Even that much would slow the war ponies.

In summer they would fly up to the Cimarron River in one full day of hard riding from sunrise to sunrise. Now even with two horses it would be a long struggle.

16

Before midday on the first morning, one war pony skidded going down a slight gully and broke its leg. Before the animal had stopped its scream of pain and fury, the warrior had slipped off his back and sliced his throat open with his knife. The animal was left kicking his way to death as they moved on. Now that warrior must risk his best war pony on the trip.

By mid afternoon the snow slacked off, then quit. The horses moved into an area where they had less snow and soon it was no more than hock deep.

"Your magic is so strong it can turn back a snowstorm!" Four Fingers called to Yellow Dog. The taller of the two smiled. He had performed a special ritual before he left. A compact with the Great Spirit, a dedication that all he did would be favorable in the eyes of the Great Spirit.

He now must be the perfect warrior, the perfect Cheyenne. The Great Spirit would be watching him closely during this raid. Nothing must spoil it!

The second day they stopped just across the Cimarron. They found a place where the ice had not been broken and walked their horses across it gently. Everyone made it. An ice crossing was better than wading in shoulder deep water.

That night they made a cold camp in a heavy grove of trees on the Cimarron. The first of the three ranches was less than twenty long arrow shots upstream. Then two more White Eye ranches were not far away. They would strike at dawn.

The Cheyenne slept, then rose early to put on their sacred paint and war bonnets, to decorate their bows, shields, rifles, and each to do his private ritual to gain as much magic as he could for the fight to come.

Just at dawn, the thirty braves waited in the brush where a small feeder stream wandered across the near field next to a house. These White Eyes dug up Mother Earth's hair, uprooted the grasses and small plants and then tried to plant their own grass and plants. It was not reasonable. The snow here was only a hand deep and in patches the ground blown bare by the wind.

Yellow Dog had an agreement with the warriors that they would surround the house and barn, then all attack on Yellow Dog's call of the night bird. But the young fighters could not wait. Those who had circled around by the barn saw the corral with ten horses in it and charged at once, opened the gate and with whoops of delight at their ownership of the animals, drove them out of the corral. At once the rest of the band charged toward the buildings.

A White Eye pulling overall straps over his shoulder ran out of the small frame house. His bare feet slapped against the snowy ground. He saw the Indians and fired his shotgun at the retreating Cheyenne. By then they were out of range.

An arrow tore into the farmer's body as he turned to see what had caused the commotion in the chicken coop. The arrow sliced through his throat, cutting his windpipe in half and left him clutching his neck, gasping for breath.

Before he knew he was dying, a rifle bullet hit his chest and a second heavy lead slug tore through his lower intestine. He died as he fell backward toward the well.

A white woman screamed in terror and ran from the house when she saw her husband fall on the frozen ground. She held a rifle but did not fire it. None of the warriors fired their rifles or arrows at the woman. She was an even greater prize than the horses. Three braves rode hard to reach her first. Two of the warriors slammed their horses together and were out of the contest. The third dropped off his war pony beside the woman, knocked the weapon from her hands and caught her from behind. His hands clawed at her breasts through the thin nightdress.

A baby cried in the small house. Two warriors darted inside and moments later came back with scalps. One of long blonde hair, and the second, a smaller scalp of dark hair, was short and curly. Soon the house burst into flames and the warriors turned to the barn.

They looked for knives and the White Eye's axes, which they had come to prize greatly. Others searched for metal that was flat and could be formed into spear points and arrow heads. One brave ran out of the barn with a five foot cross cut saw with handles on both ends. He would be the envy of the rest of the tribe.

They slashed the throats of two milk cows in the barn, then the two horses were led out and the barn burned.

One warrior proudly displayed a man's felt hat. He wore it backwards, but didn't know the difference. He also wore a woman's blouse of sea blue with small ducks printed on the cloth. He made a curious sight to the other warriors. As the barn burned, they hurried toward the next ranch.

The warrior who had captured the farm woman had tied her hands together around his waist as she sat on his war pony behind him. He had two horses but he preferred that she ride with him. Then there was no chance she could escape. The snow was deeper now as they rode over a rise and down a small slope to the next ranch.

Amy Whitright could cry no more. She had screamed herself hoarse in her terror and fury. Tears had cascaded down from her eyes when she saw Bill shot down. She knew he was dead, but she had to go check. Neighbors had told them the Indian situation was well in hand in this part of Kansas.

Amy's mind spun. Everything was disjointed. She was going crazy she was sure. Numb, she felt numb. Bill was dead. The kids? Oh, dear lord what had happened to her babies?

She had seen the Indians run out of the house with the terrible bloody things that must have been hair. No! She tried to scream again but only a rasping squawk came out. Dear God, her babies. What had happened to them?

Amy shivered. Her breasts pressed tightly against the buffalo skin the warrior wore. She had on only a thin nightdress and a robe she had snatched as she left the bedroom. At least she had pushed her bare feet into her sturdy shoes. If she hadn't, by now her toes would have frozen. A stiff Kansas wind bit into her flesh.

Amy was so numb she barely felt the cold now. Bill was dead. It wasn't real. She blacked out for a moment, her mind whirling, nothing seemed natural. Bill . . . dead. Where were her babies?

She blinked and saw the Indian her arms were around. Reality slapped her hard. Her hands were inside the buffalo robe in front of the Indian and warm, but the rest of her was icy cold. Idly, and from a distance, she thought she would surely die of exposure before the heathens got where they were going.

It didn't matter. She knew what the Cheyenne did to white women. She had promised Bill if Indians attacked they would never take her alive. But it all happened so quickly she had no time to kill herself.

Her mind wandered again. She heard Milicent call. Where were her babies! "Where are they!" she screamed suddenly. The Indian turned and looked at her, then kept riding.

At least the savages had not killed her or . . . or . . . had their way with her. They had captured her so they would make her a wife or a slave. She could escape. The army was around, perhaps. Amy snorted at that idea. Ridiculous. Thinking the army might rescue her was too much to hope for.

She cried again. Bill was dead. Where were her babies?

Ahead she saw the Branocks' ranch. Already the small barn burned furiously. Some of the warriors had rushed ahead to start the attack.

One Eyed Owl, the warrior who captured Amy, had ridden slower with the three men driving the captured horses. One Eyed Owl had his prize for the trip. He would let the others claim horses if they could. The older boys, not yet warriors, were having trouble driving the horses and stopped a half mile from the ranch.

One Eyed Owl untied the woman's hands, jumped off his war pony, and pulled her down. He opened the robe and tore the soft cloth to look at her naked body. He grunted, rubbed her breasts and caught her hand when she tried to hit him. At least she had some fire, some courage. He would keep her to wife. She was a good sized woman and could work hard.

The warrior took a second buffalo robe off his war pony and draped it around the woman. She said something he didn't understand. She huddled inside the robe near the horse, waiting.

Roughly he showed her how to arrange the robe so it would cover her and keep in her body heat. Then he brought up his second war pony and lifted her on it.

"You ride," he said, knowing she would not understand him. He used strips of rawhide to tie her ankles together under the pony's belly. He fastened the rawhide lead rope from the horse's hackamore to his waist and mounted his own war pony.

A moment later he showed her how to hold on to the horse's mane so she wouldn't fall, then they rode slowly toward the three burning buildings that had until an hour ago been the Branocks' ranch. The family had lived there for five years, and Jenny had told Amy just last week that they had never had a bit of trouble with the Indians.

"They're so like children," Jenny told Amy. "So playful and sometimes wild and childish. But we've never had any trouble at all from them. I think they are mostly Cheyenne around here."

One Eyed Owl led Amy toward the ranch. The two barns, the bunkhouse and the house all burned brightly. Amy tried not to look but she saw two bodies starkly black against the snowy yard, and another by the well. A fourth lay near the bunkhouse which still had snow covering the roof.

More killing! She wailed in anger and fear. Her husband Bill was dead. She had seen him fall. Amy cried again.

Four savages laughed and cheered near a small creek just down from the house. There was less snow under the small trees there and something lay on the snowy ground. Amy turned away. It was Jenny, naked and being held down as the savages had their way with her.

Amy looked away and sobbed. She couldn't help it. This was more than she could stand. How had it happened? Last night Bill had been so loving, so wonderful. He said he wanted another son and that he would try every day for a month. He had been so gentle and he had even taken time to satisfy that terrible/wonderful urge that she always had and it was delightful. It was three o'clock before they at last got to sleep.

Then this morning Bill leaped out of bed and grabbed his overalls and shotgun and raced out the door. . . .

She started to sob and couldn't stop.

One Eyed Owl who had captured her had a jagged scar across one cheek, and it pulled down the side of his mouth. He glared at her and shouted something. She still sobbed. He moved his horse back and slapped her face so hard she almost fell off the pony. Amy gasped, her eyes went wide and she screamed at him. When she stopped screaming she realized she was no longer sobbing.

One Eyed Owl grunted and walked his horse ahead, the one behind with Amy tied on followed so the line was not tight.

Amy stared wide eyed in the morning sun. She was frantic, still in shock, and so filled with anger and terror that she thought she was losing her mind. One moment she was numb, the next in a rage that this could happen.

The savages around Jenny Branock on the ground moved away. They left her there.

Jenny was dead, Amy knew. She knew she might as well be dead, too. There was no hope, no chance, nothing to live for.

Then the rage took hold of her. Amy bellowed out her fury, kicked the surprised Indian pony in the flanks and grabbed his mane. The startled animal bolted forward past One Eyed Owl. The rawhide thong rope had weathered too many winters. It snapped where it was tied around the Indian's waist and suddenly Amy was free!

She looked back and kicked the pony again and again as she turned his head to the left and rode away from the horror that had engulfed her for the past hour and had shattered her happy life.

Chapter Two

Colonel Colt Harding put his feet on the stool in front of the small fireplace and let the warmth and the relaxation soak into his bones. This was only one of two officer quarters at Fort Dodge with a fireplace. He reveled in it. Colt stood a little over six feet tall and solid at 185 pounds. He was lean and fit with short cropped brown hair and brown eyes under heavy brows. He wore a thick, full moustache but was otherwise clean shaven.

Right now he realized he was a lucky man. He'd just finished two months of leave at Fort Leavenworth, Kansas, where he had been able to get reacquainted with his wife Doris and the kids. It had been long overdue. Then he had been assigned by General Phil Sheridan to report here to Fort Dodge in western Kansas.

The big winter campaign was coming, but not quite ready to launch. He had another few days to spend with Doris and his daughter Sadie, now six, and their adopted boy Daniel, five. It had been so long. Ever since they got married down in Texas at Fort Comfort over a year ago, it seemed like he had been constantly in the field. Now for another few days he would luxuriate in the good life of a garrison officer.

Doris came in. She was smiling and her long black hair covered her shoulders and framed her pretty face.

"It's so good to have you home!" she said suddenly. Then she was sitting on his lap, kissing his cheek, working round to his lips. She kissed him hard, then snuggled down against his shoulder.

"Right now I wish you were a supply officer with a gimpy leg and a restricted job that kept you at the fort all the time."

"A gimpy leg?" he wailed, then grinned and hugged her. "If that were true I never would have found you in that Comanche camp, remember? Now you be good or I'll auction you off to some Cheyenne I know who likes white slave women with big tits."

She bit his ear and he grinned.

"Don't talk nasty," Doris said. "Say, both the kids are having a nap. Might be a good time for us to have a small nap of our own, a no-sleeping nap."

Colt leaned back in mock surprise. "Woman, in the middle of the afternoon? What would the general's wife say?"

Doris laughed. "I don't know. But I'll tell her to get her own man, come on. I'm trying to get pregnant so you'll have to marry me."

"Damn, marrying you once wasn't enough?"

Doris sobered as they stood. She put her arms around him and drew in close. Her words choked with emotion and barely loud enough for him to hear.

"Wonderful Colt Harding. I want the two of us to have a child of our own, a small son, who will be as marvelous as his papa."

Colt pulled her toward the second bedroom in the officer's quarters. "I want a baby, too. One of our own. So what you need is to get injected once a day, every day for a month, right?"

"Or until I get the curse." She laughed softly. "Maybe even then. I have to get all of you I can while you're at home here in the fort. I never know when General Sheridan will snatch you away from me."

They closed the door and put a chair in front of it, then sat on the bed.

"I love you, Colonel Colt Harding, I love you so much most of the time it hurts."

Colt kissed her cheek. She caught his face and kissed his lips and then pulled him down on the bed on top of her.

"Now, Colonel, do your duty!" Doris said. She smiled. "I like this, me giving a full bird colonel orders."

Colt always obeyed orders, and he did so now.

That evening, just after nine o'clock, Corporal Schultz slipped into the Charlie company supply room and waited beside the door. Not two minutes later someone knocked and he opened it cautiously. Yes, she was there! He pulled open the door and the woman slipped inside.

"Schultz?" she asked in a husky voice.

Just the sound of her voice stirred his anticipation higher. It had been a whole damn year! He rubbed his crotch.

"Yeah, right. I talked to you when you brought my laundry, right, you said tonight would be fine. I even paid in advance, two damn dollars."

"Right. You got a place?"

The supply room was secure, had no windows and only one door. Schultz had made sure of that. Now he bolted the door and pushed a chair under the knob just in case, then he lit a lamp and as the yellow glow slowly filled the supply room, he looked at his prize for the evening.

The light showed a woman in her twenties, not slender, but not fat either, a solid, "pleasingly plump" girl with large breasts. She wore a print dress and Schultz guessed little else.

30

She had blonde hair that hadn't been washed for some time, and had not known a comb or brush for days.

She was not a pretty girl, but her complexion was clear and her eyes a dull green with flecks of brown. She coughed slightly and frowned.

"So?"

"So you're Peggy? Good. Right over here. I've set up a cot with four blankets on it."

"Be better on the floor. I fell off a fucking cot like that once and damn near broke my butt."

Schultz chuckled. "We don't want that to happen. The floor it is." He lifted the blankets off the cot and spread them on the floor. By that time Peggy had unbuttoned the front of the print dress and began lifting it off over her head.

Schultz knelt on the floor watching the unveiling. He was right, she wore nothing under the dress. If she had a coat she left it in the company orderly room.

"Glory!" Schultz said. "Now there is a hell of a lot of woman and the biggest damn tits I ever seen! I mean that, so help me."

She looked at him. "So, you taking your pants off or just flippin' your short stick outa your fly?"

"Pants off," Schultz said. "Damn shirt too.

We won't freeze for a few minutes." That reminded him that the supply room was unheated. The temperature outside was just over freezing with a storm expected soon from the looks of the clouds just at dusk over to the west.

He pulled off his clothes and dropped beside her. She sat on the blankets, drew her dress over near her and looked at him.

"How do you want it, love?"

Twenty minutes later, Cpl. Schultz had collapsed on his back on the blankets, gasping for breath.

"God but you are wild. You love it, don't you? You like it better than any man. You do it and still get paid for it. Now that's one fucking good arrangement!"

Peggy had pawed at her dress for a minute, then sat up and Schultz barely saw her before he closed his eyes. He sucked in enough breath to feed his starved cells. He knew it was the longest and best climax he had ever experienced. She knew how to put him off and off and off and the pressure had kept building until he thought he was going to die!

Schultz opened his eyes as he sensed her over him. He looked at her just in time to see her hand dart down toward his belly. Then the pain came, the stabbing, burning, hot branding iron kind of pain that he had felt

32

only once before when he had been shot in the side with that damn Cheyenne arrow.

"My god, you stabbed me!" Schultz roared. He started to lift up just as the woman's doubled up right fist smashed into his jaw three times, slamming him back to the blanket and nearly knocking him out.

Then she used the knife again.

"Bastard!" she said softly. "Whoring bastard!" She stabbed him again, the slender three inch blade sank into his belly up to the hilt and she ripped it out sideways bringing a scream of raw agony from the half conscious man.

She pushed her hand over his mouth to muffle his voice, then she hit him again on the jaw and his eyes went glassy. He came back to consciousness a moment later when her slender, razor-like knife began to work on his genitals.

Corporal Schultz tried to scream but now he found a gag across his mouth and his hands tied together on his stomach. He tried to roll over but as he tightened the muscles in his belly to move, the pain hit him so hard he passed out again.

Peggy knelt beside the man, the knife doing her will as it slashed again and again. Blood flowed onto the army issue blankets turning them almost black in places. The man came in and out of consciousness, but Peggy didn't notice. She had a ritual to perform, a routine, and she went through it drawing as much pain and suffering from the whoring corporal as she could.

When his breathing turned shallow and almost stopped, she refused to be cheated. She took the knife again and slashed twice across his throat, cutting both carotid arteries, sending long spurts of fresh blood almost to the ceiling until the pressure failed and Cpl. Schultz died in twenty seconds as the lack of blood supply starved his brain and shut down vital centers.

Peggy knelt there beside him for a moment, blinked back an unshed tear and got up. She wiped the blood off her breasts and arms, then slipped into her dress. She scrubbed the knife clean on the man's shirt before she blew out the lamp and went out the door into the Company C orderly room. She slid into her coat she had left over a chair and eased open the door leading outside toward the parade ground.

She saw no one in the frosty Kansas night. Peggy slipped out the door leaving it so it would lock, then walked quickly down the company street to the small quarters that had been assigned to married enlisted men. No one saw her. She knew where the interior guards were posted and moved so they would not see her.

A few minutes later she opened the door to her quarters and went inside, locked it, and looked up as her husband came out of the bedroom with a lamp.

Melvin Fowler was a small man with a paunch from too many good dinners. He had a slightly red complexion, brown hair and long sideburns but no moustache or beard. Small, close set eyes squinted at her in the dim lamp light.

"Damn, took you long enough. Them fucking officers want laundry done any time of the day or night." Pvt. Melvin Fowler stared at his wife a minute. She looked the same as always. Face that had been sat on, big boobs and a pile driving ass that could milk him for every last bit of juice.

"Come on, I got to get to bed. Hard day tomorrow. Evidently we're getting ready for a march."

"You going?"

"Hell no, I'm in Fort Supply. I just get the troopers ready with the gear to go out and get their asses shot off." He yawned. "Damn, past my bedtime. Hey, how about biscuits and gravy for breakfast?"

"Gravy? Made out of what, that damn ration salt pork?"

"Yeah. Forget it."

"I have."

Five minutes later Peggy slid into bed, blew out the lamp and turned her back to Melvin. He knew the signs. Not tonight. Hell, he'd use her if he wanted to! Melvin sighed. He didn't feel like a fight tonight. Tomorrow for sure.

Peggy closed her eyes, forgot about the man on the bloody blanket and went to sleep in two minutes and didn't wake up until morning.

Col. Duffy Erhard shrugged but Colt could tell he wasn't pleased.

"Yes, Colonel Harding, I appreciate your position. All I know is when General Sheridan heard about the problem, he said you would be glad to help out. I don't have any officer here who knows anything about investigating a murder. Phil says you're a crackerjack at it."

"I got lucky at another post, that was all." Colt kicked at the desk leg and shook his head. "Damn, I guess an order is an order even round about. You say it happened last night?"

"Yes, in the C Company supply room. Usually that whole place is locked up tight. Somebody had a key or knew how to get in there, and that knowledge got him killed. No, not just killed, you better come take a look. The body is over at Doctor Wilshire's poor folks hospital place."

Ten minutes later Colt pulled the sheet back over the cold body of Cpl. Hans Schultz, but left his face uncovered.

"That's pure hatred. Somebody in a total rage did this. I want this man's service records, any reports on him, and I want to talk to his company commander and his closest command sergeant." Colt looked at Company C's first sergeant who took the orders and nodded.

"Where will you be, sir?"

"Check with your company commander. I'd like to use his office this morning if it's all right."

"Yes, sir, he'll be on drill all morning."

"Fine, have him and those other men in his office within twenty minutes."

Colt stared at the dead corporal's face. It was unmarked.

"This Cpl. Schultz. Did he run a gambling game of any sort? Did he loan money at high rates? Did he smuggle guns to the Indians?"

Col. Erhard shook his head. "I didn't even hear about him until this morning, so he hasn't been in any real trouble on the post in the last year since I've been here. I review all court martials. I don't think you'll find he was a troublemaker."

"You have a killing anything like this since you've been here?"

"No. One drunken brawl and a knifing, that's been about it. Most of these men are too busy to fight among themselves."

Twenty minutes later, Colt sat in the company commander's office of Charlie company and talked with a Sergeant Ormley.

"Yes sir, he was in my infantry squad. I used him as my assistant squad leader sometimes. He was an old hand, had been in the big war, busted down from first lieutenant to corporal. Never made it any higher. Said he'd had enough of the command problems. Filling out his twenty years, I'd guess. Never a bit of trouble.

"Sure, he drank now and then, but he was a sleepy drunk. Some guys get wild and go crazy, or get mean or cry. Schultz just curled up in a ball and went to sleep."

"He never get into any big money dice or card games, Sergeant?"

"No sir. Said he was such a damn poor gambler that he learned to stay away from it. Like I say, I'm the most surprised soldier on the post. Just don't figure, sir."

"What's that, Sergeant?"

"That somebody would get crazy angry

enough to do him that way, all that cutting and the blood and then his crotch! God, I'm the one who found him this morning."

"All right, Sergeant. Do me a favor and keep your ears open. If you hear anything that might help us find the killer, please get in touch with me through your first sergeant."

The soldier saluted, did an about face and marched out of the room.

The man's Company Commander wasn't much more help.

"Colonel, I've only had Charlie company for two months. I didn't know the man as well as I should, but I had no special reason to single out Schultz. He was a good soldier, never got into trouble, never did anything outstanding. He was there, one of the men in the machine. I'm sure you know what I mean, sir."

Colt walked to the window and looked out at the skiff of snow falling now and starting to cover the parade ground.

"I'm afraid I do, Captain, and we both know that is not the best way to run a company. An old sergeant of mine in the Civil War told me the only way to do the job right was to know every man by name and by sight. He said you've got to know them by sight even from behind!

"Captain, I'd suggest you get to know your men better. It could help save your life and theirs in the next fight we have with the Cheyennes."

"Yes, sir."

Colt spent the next hour going over the service record on Cpl. Hans Schultz. It was sketchy. Part of it had been lost along the line somewhere. His Civil War service had been well thought of by his superiors when he had been an officer. There wasn't a single court-martial or reprimand in his record.

Still, he was dead and someone with a gut full of hatred had vented some of that anger on his body before he was dead. His throat had been cut last to kill him. The rest of the stabbings and slashings had been done before he died.

That much was easy. A cut won't bleed after the heart stops pumping blood. The torture was committed before Schultz died.

Colt closed the jacket, tucked it under his arm and took out a pad of paper. He wrote down everything that he had learned about the case today.

Damn little.

He learned a lot of things that would do him no good. He had, in fact, eliminated most of his possible leads and points to find suspects. He now had no suspects, no angles to use to find in the killer, and absolutely no leads to who might have done the terrible deed.

The light snow continued to fall as Colt walked across the parade ground toward Fort Dodge headquarters.

General Philip Sheridan had come into the fort yesterday and had been busy setting up a field headquarters for himself in a section of former officer quarters adjacent to the fort offices. As Colt approached the unpainted wooden buildings, a Second Lieutenant hurried out of one and called to him.

"Colonel Harding?"

"Yes, Lieutenant?"

"Sir, begging your pardon, but General Sheridan wishes to inquire if you would have time in your busy investigation to spare him a few moments."

Colt grinned. "Lieutenant, as you know, that's Phil Sheridan's way of saying, 'get your ass right over here.' Where is the General?"

"This way, sir."

General Philip Henry Sheridan looked up from a desk stacked with papers. He was an unlikely looking military hero. He was shorter than average with arms too long for his body. Usually he wore any part of uniform he grabbed, preferring old, mismatched and rumpled sets of clothes.

Colt had been disappointed when he first met Sheridan, but soon he was caught up in the man's raw military ability, his talent, his

41

genius. Forgotten was the slightly odd shaped head and the widow's peak of black hair.

A New York lawyer had invited the general to dinner one night and he reported Sheridan to be: ". . . a stumpy, quadrangular, little man, with a forehead of no promise, and hair so short that it looks like a coat of black paint. But his eyes and mouth show great force."

General Sheridan looked up at Colt and grinned. "Thought you'd like the little job I gave you. Christ, did you see that body?"

"Yes, sir. My favorite army work, playing detective."

"You're damn good at it. In between times, I want you to stay current on what we're setting up for the winter campaign."

He pointed to a map of the general area south of the Arkansas River all the way through the panhandle of Texas.

"You know we've been keeping the pressure on the hostiles, trying to drive them into the reserves set aside for them, or forcing them to fight. Sometimes it works."

His finger stabbed at the map.

"We've had columns in the field through October. Colonel Custer has been working Medicine Lodge Creek and the Big Bend of the Arkansas, but found little.

"Lt. Col. Bradley swept along the Republican. We've been trying to fight the

Cheyennes, Arapahoes and Sioux but keep the Kiowas and Comanches neutral, at least for the time being. I sent General Hazen to meet with those last two tribes to talk them into coming down to Fort Cobb and go on the reserve. Didn't quite make it, but Hazen is there to accept any redskins who are tired of fighting."

Sheridan sighed and looked up at Colt. "Who the hell would slice up a man that way? His whang and his balls, all cut to mush. Christ, that must have hurt." He shook his head and looked back at the map.

"So, it's November now, and starting to snow. Now the game really starts. The Indians will be tucked into their lodges and tipis to wait out the winter the way they always do. But we're gonna surprise them this year.

"Liked your Lightning Company idea, but it won't work for a whole regiment. We don't have time to train them. We'll borrow some of your ideas. I'm going to launch a three-pronged attack on the winter camps of everybody camping in the Canadian and the Washita River Valleys.

"From the District of New Mexico, Bvt. Major General George Getty will launch a column east down the South Canadian. He'll have four mountain howitzers and 560 men.

"Major Carr will lead out a column south-

43

ward toward Antelope Hills and the head of the Red River.

"These two columns are the 'beaters,' Harding. If they find any hostiles, they will flush them downstream and into our nets. We don't expect them to find many savages up there.

"Brevet Brigadier General Alfred Sully and I will lead the biggest force of all, from eight hundred to a thousand men, including Custer's men.

"Custer and Sully have set up Camp Supply on the North Canadian a hundred miles almost due south of here. We'll gather there with Colonel Crawford's just called-up Kansas Nineteenth Volunteer Cavalry.

"From there on we butt heads with any winter-camped Indians we find. If they aren't at Fort Cobb now, they are determined to be hostiles and fair game for our cannon and rifle."

"Just where do I fit into this picture?" Colt asked. "I want to be along on the push."

Sheridan grinned. "I like to see an old war horse start to paw the ground," he said. "I'll keep you in reserve to go in and regroup, or recoup, or lead a special unit where it's needed. You'll also help me keep tabs on things in the field. Damn, I wish I could have speaking tubes to every one of my senior officers the way a ship captain uses to talk to his engineer and pilot and people. Wouldn't that be fine?"

"We should set up a field telegraph line the way General McClellan did at Mechanicsville from his command headquarters during the Civil War."

"It worked. But we don't have the time, the line, or the money. So we'll use runners, the best riders you can find in the cavalry units."

He looked at Colt. "But before we leave here you have a few days. See what you can do to help out Duffy Erhard and his murdered corporal. He's shitting shingles over it."

Colt grinned. "I've got nothing to go on, but I'll take another run at it."

"All we can ask," Sheridan said, but already his finger was tracing the Washita River down toward Fort Cobb.

Chapter Three

Black Kettle sat on his best war pony. The animal looked at him with what the chief thought was surprise. The two of them had not taken a ride for a long time. The pony had grown older, right along with Black Kettle.

The snow was only hock deep and for that the Cheyenne was glad. It would make the 80 mile ride to Fort Cobb easier. Short Robe rode up on his spotted pony and silently the two friends began their ride south along the Washita.

Little Robe had not been able to talk any braves into making the ride with him. Most of his friends were still on the raid north into Kansas. The others did not trust the long knives, did not want to go anywhere near Fort Cobb and the dreaded "reserve" even though the White Eyes promised that they would be fed and perhaps even shelter provided.

The two friends rode steadily. They would need two days to make the trip, but Black Kettle knew he had to go. He would offer to bring his entire band into the reserve, then with the way clear, he would return and hold a council to present his plan and his arguments in favor of the move. Then as many as he could persuade would be led southward.

The snowfall had been lighter than predicted but still it was cold. Black Kettle drew his buffalo robe tighter around him. The snow flakes he had seen fall yesterday were still on the cold banks of the Washita. He knew the vision was true. Visions from the Great Eagle were always correct. He would die before this snowfall now on the Washita had melted.

Quickly he hoped for a long and cold winter, so he might live out more of his days. It seemed unfair that his life hung on the whim of the weather. A bright warm sun might come and be unseasonably warm, resulting in his last day.

He brushed aside such thought and concentrated on what he would say to his Cheyenne band when he returned. How could he persuade them that the old ways, the ways of their fathers, and grandfathers, and their grandfathers, were dead and dying, that they must face the threat — the fact that the White Eyes had stolen their ancient lands.

The worst part was that war with the White Eyes was suicide. Their entire tribe, the whole Cheyenne people, could be massacred in such a war. Then there would be no future for any of them.

Far better to risk the unknown, risk the good will of the Great White Father in Washington, than to fight to the death of every one of The People!

The two friends rode the banks of the Washita without talking. It was a route they had taken many times before over the years as they moved along the river from one camp to another. They passed through and near the camps of many other bands, many of the Cheyenne Nation, more of Arapaho, Kiowa and Comanche. But this was not a time of war. Winter was the time of rest, of peace, of renewal.

When the great black hawk of night descended over the land with its wings spread wide blotting out the sun, the two Cheyenne found the best shelter nearby. It was a rock overhang that had been washed out by the raging spring floods of the Washita.

Many years ago some Indians had dug it out even more until it was a shallow cave eight feet deep and now well away from the main course of the stream.

Little Robe gathered dead wood from high water marks on the brush and soon had a fire going from a live coal he had carried in a small tin box filled with sand. The sand kept the coal alive and a tiny hole in the tin allowed enough air to get in to maintain the glow.

The fire warmed the two Cheyenne better than they had been all day. They huddled around the new fire, and then moved back as they warmed and the coals built up. They ate from a roll of pemmican and chewed on buffalo jerky.

"What will we find at Fort Cobb?" Little Robe asked.

"Soldiers, and many horses, a few tipis built of wood with floors and open places with a substance you can see through. It's the White Eye world. We must be firm and proud, yet willing to bend to their ways."

"Perhaps I'm too old to change my ways, Black Kettle. Maybe I should stay and fight and die with The People."

"No!" Black Kettle spoke sharply. "We both know the White Eyes are not gods, are not perfect. Many of them are cruel and evil and kill us for the sport of it. Yet many are kind and gentle and good.

"We both survived Sand Creek when the Pony Soldiers attacked us even though we showed the U.S. flag and had agreed to come to their reserve. Now we will try again. I might not survive another surprise attack such as Sand Creek. When I die, who will lead my band, my people?"

They talked of many things late into the night. At last they heaped the fire with the rest of the dry wood they had gathered, pulled their buffalo robes around them and went to sleep.

It was the third day before they rode into Fort Cobb. There were fewer of the White Eyes there than Black Kettle had expected. A sentry had called out when he saw them at the edge of the clearing, and soon an officer and six mounted soldiers came riding toward them.

Black Kettle had lifted a pole with a white cloth on it, and he and Little Robe rode steadily forward on their ponies. The Pony Soldiers pulled to a stop in front of them and the officer came forward, his hand on his revolver holster.

Black Kettle and Little Robe stopped and Black Kettle gave the Indian sign for hello and welcome. The Pony Soldier did not know the signing. Black Kettle then said the one White Eye word that he knew. "Surrender."

The officer nodded and said something, then pointed to their bows and arrows across their backs. They had brought them with the hope they might find some small game along the way for a filling supper. Black Kettle considered what the Pony Soldier wanted, then took all of his arrows and gave them to the officer.

This satisfied him, and Little Robe did the same. Then the officer with the yellow stripe down his blue pants legs, led them forward into the arrangement of buildings and to one with a sign with White Eye words on it over the door.

The Officer said something, but the Indians did not understand. He led them inside and the six Pony Soldiers took the hackamores of the Indian ponies and looked at them curiously.

Inside, the officer talked with a large man with a full beard who had stars on his shoulders. "Welcome," the bearded White Eye Star Soldier said in Cheyenne.

Black Kettle looked up and smiled. "Then you speak our tongue. Good."

But the General shook his head and went back to English. A moment later, an Indian in white eye clothes came into the room and frowned at Black Kettle.

"So, my friends the Cheyenne have come to their senses and will move to Fort Cobb. It is good. I am Bear Tooth and I speak enough of your language so we can talk."

"Tell the White Eye Star Soldier we are here to learn. We must know what we will have, how and where we will live, what we are to be given here on the reserve before we agree to come in."

Bear Tooth nodded and spoke in English to the star bearer. He listened, looked at Black Kettle and nodded, then talked again in the white eye tongue.

Bear Tooth turned to Black Kettle. "The White Eye General understands, and he will show you all that we have here that will be used to help the Cheyenne who come to the reserve. Come now and he will show you how well and safe and warm and fed the Cheyenne will be during the long winter and then . . . forever."

The tour was extensive. The two Cheyenne stared with disbelief at the large wooden building filled to the rafters with sacks of corn and grains. It could be pounded and ground into flour to make all kinds of foods, Bear Tooth told them. There was another place kept dark but filled with sacks of potatoes. Bear Claw explained that was a root that could be eaten in many ways and was a staple of the diet of many white eyes.

Most impressive were the pens and pastures where they saw more than five hundred of the steers, or White Eye's buffalo.

"The steers will be given out as needed to the Cheyenne," Bear Tooth said.

"They are not as fat and sturdy as the buffalo," Little Robe said.

"But these are cattle that can be raised and

herded," Bear Claw said. "These cattle will not die out on the plains as the White Eyes move into the hunting grounds."

"I like buffalo better."

Black Kettle grimaced. "Yes, so do I, but these White Eye's buffalo are better than no meat at all. We'll learn to like them."

Back in the office, the soldier general stood next to a round black stove that was hot from a fire that burned inside it. He held out his hands to warm them and spoke as Bear Tooth interpreted.

"All of this could be yours, if you had signed the treaty. Now I can't accept the Cheyenne into the reserve. The great General Sheridan has said that the Cheyenne did not sign the treaty and that they gave up their right to peace. I'm sorry that I can't welcome you and your band. The only thing you can do is travel to where the great General Sheridan lives and talk to him. I'm sorry, it's the best I can do."

A half hour later the two Cheyenne rode their war ponies out of Fort Cobb and turned north along the Washita. The soldier general had offered to give them a noon meal at the big building, but they had refused. Black Kettle would not eat a man's food who would not be his friend.

The Cheyenne sighed as they retraced their

route back along the Washita. Now there was no reason to speak to the council of peace, of going into the reserve. Now the Cheyenne and the army were enemies again.

Black Kettle remembered the Giant Eagle's vision about his death. At least Sand Creek was behind him. Such a tragic mistake could not be made again by the Pony Soldiers.

Black Kettle cast his eyes on the snowy ground in front of him, tightened the buffalo robe around his face and urged his war pony forward. Every step took them that much farther from danger of the Pony Soldiers at Fort Cobb.

Black Kettle knew that he had to see the great General Sheridan, but how did he find him? If he did learn where he was, how did an enemy Indian walk into the General's camp without being shot a dozen times by the Pony Soldier rifles?

Amy Whitright's dash for freedom lasted less than a hundred yards. One Eyed Owl charged after her, called to the pony which slowed, and he caught them almost at once. He slapped her face hard and she cried out in pain.

The cry surprised One Eyed Owl. Indian women never let him know when he hurt them. Amy cried again, knowing for certain that her chances of escaping were over, that she would be raped and worked and humiliated and tortured. She would be a slave. Amy knew that she would be better off dead.

Curiously, One Eyed Owl did not hit her again. He touched her cheek gently where he had hit her and spoke rapidly to her in a language she didn't understand. Then he used some Indian sign language she couldn't fathom. At last he shrugged, retied the rawhide rope to his waist, and they moved with the rest of the band toward the third ranch.

One Eyed Owl left her tied hand and foot, secured to the war pony which he tied to a tree well away from the third ranch.

Two younger boys stayed to watch the captured horses as the warriors swooped down on the next ranch. It was the Johnsons. Amy knew Mary Anne as such a pretty little thing, black flashing eyes, dark hair, a slender woman of about thirty who was always so cheerful. Then Amy tried to think of something else. She didn't want to think what was happening to Mary Anne.

The raiders came back an hour later. Amy could smell the smoke of the burning buildings. She didn't even look in that direction. Four more warriors wore pieces of clothing from the ranch. One had on a cavalry blue shirt under his buffalo robe.

Amy saw that there were no more slaves, no prisoners. She blinked back a dry tear for the memory of Mary Anne and kicked the pony into motion when the Indian came and untied the animal.

They had captured almost eighty horses at the ranch. The Johnsons had run a large cattle operation, and needed lots of horses for the ranch work and cattle drives. The added number of horses slowed down the party but the warriors were all happy. Some of them were drunk from whiskey found at the ranch.

That night they camped in a draw out of the wind. There was still two hands of snow on the ground, but the happy warriors didn't even notice it. More whiskey passed around and half the men were drunk.

One Eyed Owl did not drink. He moved to Amy, untied her ankles and walked her up the draw fifty yards and under some trees. There was almost no snow there. He unfolded a blanket he had stolen at the ranch and spread it on the ground. He said something to her and when she didn't move, he gently pushed her down on the blanket.

"No!" Amy said. Then she frowned. He was going to have his way with her no matter what she did. He was larger and much stronger. If she fought, he would hit her. She was a widow, she had no loyalty to any man. This

Indian was just another man. Slowly she rationalized her position and when he pulled the buffalo robe open, she did not object.

Amy submitted to him and realized that he was only a male wanting his release. It came quickly and he grunted and came away from her. She sat up and pulled her night dress and robe back in place and then the buffalo fur robe which kept her from freezing.

One Eyed Owl nodded, fondled her breasts inside the robe and nodded again. He said something, then lifted her to her feet. He folded the blanket and led her back near the others. He showed her where to lay down, gave her the blanket, and did not tie her. He seemed to know that she would not try to escape.

Amy wondered how he had figured that out. They were in the middle of the wilderness. There were six inches of snow on the ground. She probably couldn't steal a horse. Even if she did get one, she had no idea in what direction to ride. And if she did ride away, she would leave a plain trail in the snow.

She tucked the warm buffalo robe around her, pulled her legs up to form a ball and tried to go to sleep. For a brief moment she wondered what would happen if she became pregnant. If she needed to, she could claim she was pregnant when captured. A day would make no difference. That meant she had to be rescued. Right then there didn't look like a chance in the world that could happen.

Amy Whitright went to sleep remembering the forceful yet still gentle way the Indian had made love to her. She could remember times when her husband had been rougher. Amy shivered, then settled down. She would survive. She would survive!

Once during the night Amy woke, groggy and cold. She pulled the robe around her and tucked it in, then saw someone lying near her and pushed back until she touched the person there to combine their body heat. She saw it was the Indian who had taken her so gently. He seemed to push against her and again she slept.

The morning came cold and with a light snow falling. They brushed themselves off, and went to their horses at once. It would be a long day again and the Indians wanted to be back with their women in their own warm tipis that night.

Governor Samuel J. Crawford, Commanding Colonel of the Nineteenth Kansas Volunteer Cavalry of some 353 men, was ordered to muster his troops into Federal service in October. His rank was full Colonel and he was told to march his cavalry to Camp Supply, Indian Territories, arriving there "on or about" November 10, 1868.

The march went fine the first few days, then the troopers rode into heavy snowfall along the Cimarron River thirty miles from Camp Supply. They knew the Camp was almost due south of Fort Dodge on the North Canadian River.

The scouts were unfamiliar with the territory and soon the entire troop was hopelessly lost in the snow-choked gorges of the Cimarron. New scouts were sent out to determine their position and find a new route of travel.

At Camp Supply, Lieutenant Colonel Custer and Lieutenant Colonel Sully waited anxiously for the arrival of Colonel Crawford. The two light colonels worried about full Colonel Crawford taking command due to his higher permanent rank. They each worried about it separately, then decided to act.

While the various pieces of the Washita battle fell into place, General Sheridan paced his office back in Fort Dodge making sure that every part of his command was finely tuned and ready for a winter fight. Every man had all the winter clothing then available, including the heavy, long blue, double breasted overcoat with twin rows of buttons on the front.

General Sheridan wished they had better boots for the troops that would turn away the slush and snow, but none were approved yet by the quartermaster in Washington D.C.

Sheridan waited for word that Colonel Crawford had arrived at Camp Supply so he could go down and get the attack on the hostiles moving. Word did not come. Two, three, then four more days went by.

Colt Harding luxuriated in the days with his family, spending as much time as he could with them, playing with little Danny, listening as Sadie showed him how well she was learning to read. Her schooling had been spotty so far, and Colt was determined that she be as well educated as possible.

He had made absolutely no headway on the murder. There were none of the dead man's friends who had any inkling that he was mixed up in anything dangerous. Quickly Colt ruled out any gambling, drinking bouts, service connected enemies, or any type of illegal activity. He was at a standstill.

Colt reported this fact to Colonel Erhard who snorted and slapped a riding crop on his desk.

"I've got a murderer running loose right here on my post! Gods, man! I can't permit that! I have to find the culprit, try him and hang him. My whole command authority is at stake here. This killer has cut down a fine soldier, and I intend to find him and bring him to justice!"

"Might I suggest you call in the Pinkertons, Colonel. I've done all I can. I have no leads, nothing to work with. The killer must be someone who the victim knew only slightly, or perhaps not at all. That means we have absolutely no valid avenue of investigation."

Colonel Erhard slumped in his chair. "Damnit, Harding, I know all that. You also know the army won't authorize Pinkerton's fee for this kind of thing. Forget I yelled at you. Sheridan is pacing his office these days, see if you can help him. I'll keep track of anything here that might help."

"Then I'm released from this duty for a while?"

"Yes, but just don't get yourself shot full of arrows. We still have to clean up this thing."

Colt saluted and almost ran out of the Fort Commander's office.

Chapter Four

Camp Supply was simply that in 1868, a supply depot designed to resupply a thrust down the rivers toward Fort Cobb and rout the hostiles. There had been no thought of permanent buildings or barracks or offices.

Sibley tents supplied most of the protection for the officers. For the men it was like a constant field exercise.

Lieutenant Colonel George A. Custer, reduced in rank from his two stars earned in the Civil War with the army's reorganization, had brought to Camp Supply eleven troops of his Seventh Cavalry along with five infantry companies.

Custer was chafing for a fight. He was never a popular man in the army, especially with his troops. He knew that the army called him flamboyant and undisciplined. He fully realized that many called him a fool and a bad commander.

But he calmly pointed out that he had graduated from West Point 34th in a class of 34. Yet during the Civil War, he joined the cavalry and was promoted from First Lieutenant to Brigadier General between July 1862 and July of 1863. He was twenty-three years old. It was the fastest promotion ever recorded in U.S. military history.

When he was twenty-five, he became a Major General with two stars and took over the command of three army divisions.

Custer was an excellent horseman — some said the best in the army — a natural athlete who stood nearly six feet tall, had broad shoulders, and blonde hair that fell to his shoulders in curls.

Most of Custer's troops disliked and feared him. They distrusted him. He demanded absolute discipline from his troops, yet he himself was sloppy and unkempt. He pushed his troops just beyond their endurance, then urged them on to greater efforts.

Now, in Fort Supply, his main worry was Bird Colonel Crawford, the politician/soldier coming with the Kansas Volunteer Cavalry of 350 men. Crawford had a permanent rank that bested Custer's Lieutenant Colonel leaves.

Would Crawford move in and take over as commander by reason of his rank? Undoubtedly.

"The upstart!" Custer roared to no one. "The political bastard thinks he can sweep in here and take this command away from me!"

Two tents away, Lieutenant Colonel Sully was having much the same struggle. He at last resolved the matter in his own mind. He issued a written order to all troops naming himself as Commander of Camp Supply and its troops due to his brevet rank of Brigadier General.

Custer accepted the paper from an orderly and stared at the signature and the content for only a moment.

"Ridiculous!" Custer roared. He called in his orderly and dictated a new order saying that he was relieving Lieutenant Colonel Sully of command of Camp Supply and assuming command himself since he had a brevet rank of Major General.

For almost a week, the troops sat or lay in their small pup tents in the snow as it grew deeper and deeper. The officers' tents had to be shaken free of snow every few hours, and soon there was over a foot on the level.

The two Commanders of the supply depot sat and waited. There was no word from Colonel Crawford. He was already four days overdue. Custer and Sully stared at each other and made hateful faces, but there was nothing to be done to resolve the matter until General Sheridan came from Fort Dodge, a hundred miles through the Kansas and Indian Territories snowscape to the north.

It was November 21, 1868 when General Sheridan rode into Camp Supply in the middle of a snowstorm. He was welcomed by the whole camp who knew that now that the General was here, something would be done. One way or the other, they didn't care. The troops and officers alike were tired of sitting in the snow and waiting.

General Sheridan moved into the Sibley tent that had been waiting for him. The Sibley was conical in shape and had a smoke flap at the top that acted as a draft control. The tent was supported by a single pole and the sides were staked down to the ground. As with most Sibley tents, this one included a Sibley stove, a conical affair of sheet iron used for both cooking and heating.

Colonel Colt Harding helped the General get situated, then found space for his blankets in one of the officer tents. Almost before the snow had melted from General Sheridan's overcoat, Custer and Sully were both standing in his tent presenting their own case to be Commander of the force.

General Sheridan listened to the two men present their arguments, based almost solely on rank and higher rank. He preened his thick black moustache and stared at the two men.

"Sully, Custer will command. You better

get back to your district headquarters and mind the store."

George Custer had been Sheridan's strong right arm more than once before. In the Civil War, Sheridan had pillaged the Shenandoah Valley, but it was Custer and the Seventh who led the way. When Sheridan stopped Robert E. Lee's final retreat, it had been Custer's division that smashed the Confederate cavalry and charged on forward over Lee's chopped up infantry. Now George Custer would lead the way for Sheridan again.

Sheridan was told that Colonel Crawford had still not arrived with his Kansas Volunteer Cavalry. The short, long armed little General paced his tent. He did not like to be kept waiting. He endured the hold up for the rest of the day and the next. On the third morning he told Custer they would wait no longer, they would move down the Washita without Colonel Crawford.

On the morning of November 23, 1868, a long line of nearly 800 men rode down the Washita. They were followed by a string of supply wagons. The Regiment was on the move.

A foot of wet snow covered the ground, and again it was snowing. The snowfall continued throughout the day.

When Sheridan had ridden in, he and his

small party had crossed a wide trail of a raiding party of unshod Indian ponies heading north toward Kansas. All they had to do was back track the trail and it should lead directly to the renegades' camp.

However, three days later, fresh snow had covered the trail, so Custer had to send out scouts and proceed slowly in the direction he believed the Cheyenne would be — downstream on the Washita River.

By the end of four long, hard days of marching through snow that tired the horses and exhausted the infantry, Custer's scouts found a village of Indians on the Washita.

Custer did not know what tribe they were, but any Indians in this area were renegades who had chosen not to go to the reserve at Fort Cobb. They were fair game.

Custer took his time, moved his troops into position on all four sides of the camp, and when the sun came up November 27th, he planned to launch the attack.

Custer had no idea what tribe it was or how many warriors were there. He had counted 51 tipis along the river. The bugles blared the charge call for the cavalry, and the band blared out *Garry Owen*. But soon the instruments froze and the bandsmen couldn't touch lips to mouthpiece.

Custer's men and the infantry fell on the

hapless Cheyenne camp of Black Kettle from four directions.

Colonel Colt Harding attached himself to Able Troop of the Seventh and charged in with them from the land side of the north. It was the same scene Colt had been a part of too often. Warriors rushed from their tents, some in buckskins, some with robes over their naked bodies. A few found rifles and pistols. Some snatched up bows and arrows and lances at the flaps of their tipis and fired at the onrushing blue shirted soldiers.

Colt shot a warrior running for the horses. He saw someone else leap from the tipi and almost fired but saw it was an Indian woman with two children. He let them pass. They rushed through the foot deep snow to the river, broke the ice and waded downstream in the freezing water up to their waists.

Rifles and pistols cracked and roared from all over the string of tipis along the Washita. Colt saw a white woman rush out, then dart back into one tipi. He leaped off his horse and charged into the lodge, his pistol up and cocked.

In the dank dim light of the tipi, he saw the woman cowering against the far wall. An Indian woman raised a knife and was running at the white woman.

Colt fired, his bullet hitting the squaw in

the side, knocking her away from the white woman, killing her instantly.

Colt saw the scene now. Two other white women lay on the floor of the tipi, their throats slashed. The white woman captive came away from the wall, her eyes wide. She looked at Colt, then ran to him, threw her arms around him and broke into sobs.

"Dead!" she wailed. "Both of them dead! I ran outside but then I saw all the shooting."

The woman couldn't go on. Colt pulled her arms from around him.

"At least we saved one of you. Now we'll look outside and see what we can do to get you to a safer place."

She held onto his arm as they went toward the tipi opening. A blue shirted soldier leaped into the opening, his rifle up.

"No, soldier!" Colt barked.

The man lowered his rifle.

"This one is cleared, trooper, move on," Colt ordered.

The man nodded, reversed himself and ran outside.

Colt slid through the tipi flap opening and looked around. The cavalry had moved on downstream, clearing tipis, herding women and children into one area where they could be guarded.

Several bodies lay around the tipis. He saw

two soldiers down and wounded or dead. Five warriors lay crumpled in the snow.

A cavalry Corporal rode by and Colt bellowed at him. He whirled his mount and came back.

"Corporal, take this woman back to the rear to a point of safety and remain with her. If a hand touches her, it's worth your scalp. You understand that, trooper?"

"Yes sir!"

Colt brushed loose hair out of the woman's face and smiled at her. "What's your name?"

"Oh, Amy. I'm Amy Whitright. I used to live up in Kansas. The Cheyenne . . ."

"Yes, I understand. Go with this trooper. He's your personal guard. Right, Corporal?"

"Yes, sir, Colonel!"

Colt made a step with his hands for her and she lifted up to the horse's back. She held to the soldier's shirt and he rode slowly toward the trees.

A Cheyenne brave, wounded but not dead, lifted up and aimed an arrow at the pair. Colt's .44 thundered in the sudden quiet of the camp. The Cheyenne turned, surprised at the weapon so near him, and died where he lay.

Colt waved the Corporal on.

He grabbed his mount's reins and lifted to the saddle. The firing was downstream. He rode that way. Cheyenne continued to battle from behind trees and the banks of the river.

In ten minutes the whole camp had been captured, but it would take hours to clean out the pockets of resistance. Colt moved from one to another. The men had to fight on foot, and gradually the remaining warriors were flushed out and shot or they faded away down stream.

Early in the attack, Black Kettle and his family had been roused from their beds by the sound of rifle fire. Black Kettle had kept his horse near the tipi that night fearing that something was wrong.

With the first sound of gunfire he rushed from his tipi, caught the horse and lifted his wife on board. Then he swung up himself and rode for the trees. More gunfire came from their right so they turned left and ran directly into the fire of the two hundred troopers charging in from that direction.

Black Kettle screamed at them that he was a friend. The first rifle round hit him in the shoulder and nearly knocked him from the horse. Another struck him in the chest and a third in the throat. As he fell, his wife tumbled off as well. She had taken four bullets before she hit the ground.

Nearby, Chief Little Robe died aiming his treasured six-shot pistol at a whole charging cavalry troop. He went down and died under their hooves in seconds.

Toward the downriver end of the line of tipis, Major Joel H. Elliott spotted a half dozen warriors slipping through the shallows of the Washita and rushing downstream. He shouted to fifteen mounted troopers and ordered them to follow him to capture or kill the fleeing warriors.

Major Elliott was a seasoned veteran of Indian fighting. He charged into the light brush along the Washita and passed the herd of Cheyenne horses. He was amazed at the number, nearly a thousand he guessed.

He charged ahead with his men searching for the hostiles who had escaped. After a charge of five hundred yards, he saw them running up a small gully to the left. His men splashed across the shallow Washita and charged the running Cheyenne.

As they did, twenty mounted Cheyenne warriors, six of them armed with single shot rifles, swung in behind the troopers and began picking them off.

When the Major saw the danger, he wheeled his remaining troops and tried to ride out. But he was too late. The fleeing warriors had led him into a trap. They turned and fired arrows and the surging Cheyenne warriors galloped head-on into the remaining troopers of the Seventh Cavalry.

They fought from horseback, until the Major ordered the six remaining troopers to dismount and take positions behind some heavy growth and rocks. He had a good defensive front set up. Now all he had to do was hold them off until he was missed and Custer would send a search party to rescue him.

Within five minutes the Cheyenne had infiltrated behind him and attacked from that direction, wiping out Elliott and his detachment with rifle fire before they could reposition.

Back at the main camp, the battle was over. Sheridan himself identified Black Kettle and Chief Little Robe. He had met both of them at treaty conferences.

Custer took a casualty report and found that Major Elliott was missing and Captain Louis Hamilton had been killed. Nineteen troopers had also died and he had fourteen men and officers wounded. He had captured fifty-three women and children, which by army orders he must take with him as prisoners until they could be sent to a reserve.

His men reported 103 warriors slain. Colt questioned the number. It seemed high for a village of only 51 tipis. He was sure many of the dead were women or children killed accidentally in the surge of battle. But he made no challenge of the figures.

Colt made a quick run to locate Major Elliott, but found no trace.

The battle situation was still dangerous. Pockets of Cheyenne still fought, and no organized search could be made for the missing Major and fifteen men who also could not be accounted for.

Two hours before noon, Colt noticed well armed warriors on the hills on both sides of the village. The men were mounted and had on their war paint, ready for battle.

Custer used an interpreter and questioned the captive women who at last admitted that there were other Indian camps downstream for as far as ten miles. They said winter camps had been set up by the Arapaho, Kiowa and Comanche.

Colt watched the hills and by noon he could see hundreds of armed, mounted warriors ringing Black Kettle's former camp. Custer ordered a perimeter defense drawn up.

"Here comes a charge!" a lookout called.

Thirty mounted warriors surged from a small hill leading off the Washita. Those in front had rifles. They fired and turned off in each direction, then the warriors behind them fired a flurry of arrows before also spinning off each way and retreating.

The Custer cavalry spilled eight of the attackers off their horses before they vanished through the woods up the hill and out of effective range.

As this happened, Custer had ordered the camp destroyed and all the horses shot. Fires sprang up in each tipi. The flames licked at the buffalo hide covers, ate the long poles holding up the leather, and consumed the robes and stacks of parfleches loaded with pemmican and buffalo jerky stored inside each tipi.

Men threw burned off tipi poles back into the cauldron of flames until there wasn't a stick or a pot or a robe in the camp that could be used.

Rifle fire continued for an hour as the horses and ponies were slaughtered. The final count was brought to Custer. A total of 875 Cheyenne ponies died. It would put a critical void in the Cheyenne's ability to move and to fight.

Colt and Custer and General Sheridan watched the ring of warriors on the hills. They had the high ground. Colt wondered just how many there were. Ten miles of winter camps could produce a lot of angry warriors from the three tribes. They would unite now to defend their camps and their women and children.

Custer ticked off the problems:

"We have dead and wounded to move with us. We have over 50 prisoners to watch and transport. Our supply train is a half day's ride behind us, along with our overcoats and haversacks, so we have no food. And we still don't know where Major Elliott is.

"Now we have a thousand war-painted Indian warriors ringing our position and they look anxious to die in battle."

He watched the other officers. "My teachers at West Point would say now is the prudent time to execute a cautious retrograde movement, to retreat." Custer snorted. "Damned if I'll do that. We came here to kill Indians, so let's kill the damn Indians!"

By three o'clock the troops were told to get ready to move out. Guards were assigned the prisoners. Mrs. Whitright was to ride between her corporal escort and General Sheridan. The dead were tied over their saddles and assigned to troopers to lead. The wounded who could not sit a saddle were tied into one and the line of march readied.

An hour before dusk, Custer gave the command. The band struck up a tune, the scouts moved out in front and the column swung boldly downstream with all colors flying ready to attack the next village.

Colt grinned. He was as caught by surprise as he imagined the Indian warriors on the surrounding hills must have been. They must have been certain that their show of force would mean the White Eye Pony Soldiers would retreat upstream.

There was confusion on the hills, then quickly the mounted warriors rode off at a gallop downstream. The Indians were rushing back to their villages to help defend their own.

Custer slowed the rate of march, and as soon as dusk fell, Custer ordered the troops to about face and marched at a much quicker pace upstream. He had thrown the enemy off balance by his supposed charge, now he could withdraw without any attacks or losses and get away safely.

They reached their haversacks and overcoats and moved another two hours through the dark before stopping for the rest of the night. Not a man was lost on the retreat.

Custer ordered that no tents, except one for General Sheridan, be erected. The General watched the tent go up, then sent for Mrs. Whitright who had the honor of sleeping inside that night.

Five hard marching days later, Custer led his Seventh Cavalry and the rest of the troopers proudly into Camp Supply. It was December 2, 1868, and the first Battle of Washita had been a success.

Chapter Five

The last day's ride into Camp Supply, Colt had stayed beside Amy Whitright. She had been subdued, and cried silently sometimes. Colt tried to draw her out, but she spoke little and then only enough to be polite.

At the noon break the last day, Colt found her walking back and forth in a path she had made in the snow. He stopped her and waited until she looked up at him.

"Mrs. Whitright, when we get you back to the fort, you're going to stay with my family." She started to react, but Colt held up his hand. "No, don't say anything yet. Let me explain. You may think you are uniquely unfortunate with your tragedies. I admit it must have been hard, but you're a young woman with most of your life ahead of you.

"My wife's name is Doris. I met her the first time about the same way I met you. I rescued her from a Comanche tipi, only it was in the dead of night and she had my small daughter with her and an orphan boy named Daniel. We got away from the Comanches, and a few months later I married Doris and we took in Daniel.

"I want you to know that Doris will help you however she can. We'll provide you with clothes, and find you some luggage, and if you want to go wherever any of your family is, we'll see that you have coach or train fare. Any questions?"

Tears brimmed her eyes. "How can I ever thank you! I've been so worried about what I would do, where I would go. I know the women at the fort will think of me as a ruined woman because I was a slave of the Cheyenne for three weeks. What you say is such a comfort!"

That afternoon on December 2, 1868, they rode into Camp Supply. Amy Whitright was smiling. She had taken an interest in washing as best she could, but she had left her long blonde hair in the braid down her back. She said it was easier to take care of that way out there on the trail.

Colt conferred with General Sheridan and received permission to take Mrs. Whitright on to Fort Dodge, so she could get back on her feet. He was given fifteen lightly injured troopers to serve as escort and two ambulances filled with seriously wounded.

It took them five days to make the hundred miles back to Fort Dodge through a snow covered landscape. Sometimes the Kansas winds had blown the snow away and they had level frozen ground to roll across. Sometimes they found six foot drifts and had to go around them.

They were on their last day's rations when the party pulled into Fort Dodge. The wounded were taken directly to the doctor's small hospital section and received their first real treatment in six days.

Colt hurried Amy to his own quarters and opened the door. Doris took one look at Amy and ran to her and held her in her arms. Doris did not have to be told what had happened to Amy. Her look at the long squaw dress and the winter moccasins had been enough.

Tears brimmed Doris's eyes and then both of them cried, and they vanished into the bedroom.

Shortly Doris came out and ordered Colt to draw three buckets of water and put them on the stove to heat. Then she went back into the bedroom. Colt smiled and heated the water and got down the round galvanized tub they used for bathing. He sat it beside the bedroom door, and told Doris the water was ready and that he had to report in at headquarters.

Colt checked in with Colonel Erhard. The Fort Commander looked up and rubbed his chin with his hand. They talked briefly about the success of the Washita sweep and Colonel Erhard relaxed a little. Then he bristled.

"About time you got here, Harding. We had another killing. Looks like we've got a real maniac on our hands. You better go over and talk to Doc Wilshire. He wanted to talk to you first thing. Looks like he'll be busy for a while with the wounded. How many men we lose?"

Colt told him, then he frowned. "You have a report, a file, anything on this second killing?"

Colonel Erhard handed him a file and shook his head. "Won't do you one hell of a lot of good, but you can take a look at it. Doc should be in his quarters in a couple of hours. I want you to hear what he has to say."

It was afternoon when they had arrived at Fort Dodge. By nine that night Doctor Captain Wilshire was still hard at work on the wounded. He lost one man to a serious bullet wound near his spine. He swore for five minutes, then moved on to the next trooper.

Colt had gone to the hospital to watch the medical man at work. An hour later he finished on the last man and washed his hands, then sat in his small office.

"Colonel Harding, just the man I need to see. Let's go down to my quarters. The bar service is much better there."

A short time later, Colt settled down in the living room of the fort doctor's quarters. His wife had just brought in warm cups of coffee with a shot of whiskey in them. Doc Wilshire was a tightly built man, not much over five-six, and sparse, but with energy shooting out of him like a pitch burning campfire.

"Two of them," Doc blurted. "Damndest things I ever seen. I'm not much on figuring out somebody's motives, but I'm really stumped by this pair of killings." Doc sipped the coffee and shook his head. "Damned curious. Looks like the stabbing was to make the victim helpless, wounded damn bad. Then the killer took his time slicing up the victim."

"This one have the genitals slashed as well?" Colt asked.

"Damn right! Worse than the first one. This Private was a big guy, six two, over two hundred pounds, and with the longest pecker I ever saw. Never did cut his whang off, you know, just sliced it and skinned it. Lordy, what that knife did to that poor man's scrotum and balls — I just can't tell you."

"Throat cut the same way as the first one?" Colt asked.

"Damn near identical." The medical man peaked his fingers and stared through them at Colt. "The fascinating thing to me is not how the man was tortured and killed. What I want to know is *why*. The mind is a strange device.

"We don't know much about it yet, but medicine is trying. Sure we have insane asylums where we put away people we say are too crazy to be living with the rest of us. But we really don't know who is crazy and who isn't. Not yet."

"Doctor, did you read my investigation report on the first one? He had no enemies that I could find, not even by stretching the truth and the testimony could I come up with a single reason anyone would want to kill that trooper."

"Yet there must be a tremendously powerful reason why someone did kill him." The doctor took a long pull on the hot coffee. "Now I'm coming up with a little different tack. Maybe there was no *special* reason for killing either man.

"This second man was a little more active than the first, but he didn't have any obvious enemies either. When I put the two of them together, it seems to ring a far off bell about something I heard about in medical school in New York City.

"The police found three men who were killed and they all had their right hands cut off. The three murders took place over several weeks. The police couldn't understand it.

When they finally found the killer, almost by chance, it turned out that the man had been in an accident in a mill and lost his right hand. He developed an intense hatred for anyone with a right hand, and decided he'd even up the score.

"Anyway, he killed three men before they caught him. He simply picked out random victims, got them drunk in a saloon and then chopped off their right hands before he killed them."

Colt nodded, knowing it could happen with the hundreds of thousands of people crowded together in New York City. He tried to apply the same idea here.

"Then, Doctor, you're saying these men might have been killed simply at random, with nothing in common, and not because of who they knew or enemies or what they did?"

"I'm thinking along that line, yes sir."

Colt sipped at the coffee. The doctor's wife, Martha, came in and refilled the coffee cups and the doctor added the shot of whiskey. They both pulled at the special coffee and stared at the sheet metal stove that gave off waves of heat.

Colt turned it over and over in his mind. He did not like the implications of the line of reasoning — but there was no way that he could deny the logic, or come up with a better one.

At last he put down the coffee cup and held out his hands toward the fire.

"First, Doctor, I assume that you believe the same person committed both of these torture killings."

The medic nodded.

"Then we're saying here that they *probably* were random victims, with no or little connection with each other. They were not killed for what they had done or who they were."

"Well, there is some commonality, but it's not important. They are both men, both are cavalry troopers and both are stationed here at Fort Dodge. But that can be said of the two hundred men we still have here who aren't with General Sheridan."

"Doctor, what this means is that the case is even tougher now than when I left it two weeks ago. Now we have more data that makes it harder than ever to solve the case. They are random killings by the same person who could be any one of over about 300 persons here on the post."

"I'm afraid that's about the result of my thinking. I wanted to see what you thought of my logic."

"It's perfect, even the syllogisms are perfect. The bad part is it makes my job a hundred times harder." Colt finished the coffee and stood. "Now I better sleep on this and see how it looks in the morning. I'll be in contact with you again." He picked up his hat and overcoat off the chair.

"Any idea why a man might get so crazed that he would do something like this?"

Doctor Wilshire shook his head. "Not an idea in the world. The human mind is a deep dark secret, even to us doctors."

Colt said goodnight to the medic, thanked his wife for the coffee and went out into the sub-freezing weather for his walk down the company street to his quarters. At least one small problem had been solved. He was sure that Doris would know exactly what to do and to say to Amy Whitright to make the rescued woman smile and to help build up her self-confidence again.

When Colt got back to his quarters it was nearly eleven o'clock. The kids were sleeping but Amy and Doris were still up. Colt stared in surprise at Amy. Her long blonde hair had been braided down the back when he had found her. Now it was washed and combed and brushed until it glistened around her head and shoulders like a cascading golden crown.

Her face was scrubbed and when she looked up at him she smiled her thanks.

"What a pretty lady!" Colt said at once. "We're not going to be able to let you outside for fear a whole pack of these army troopers will propose to you."

She stood and Colt saw she had on one of Doris's dresses that they had altered to fit the slightly shorter woman.

"Colonel, I can't tell you how surprised and thankful I am by all of this. A few days ago I was thinking about killing myself. Really I was. Now everything looks so much better.

"Doris tells me I can write a letter and it will go by army dispatch to the nearest post office. I have family in Ohio."

"Amy is going to stay with us for at least a month, to get readjusted and rested," Doris said. "Then if she's lucky, I'll let her go. I'm sure there'll be an army wagon train heading back to the railroad up at Fort Hays where Amy can catch the train back to Ohio."

"I agree. A few weeks of rest is called for." Colt grinned. "What a pretty lady! And what a difference from the first day I saw you come storming out of that tipi on the Washita. Amy, I'm glad I found you that day."

"Colt, you heard about the second killing?" Doris asked.

"Been talking to Doctor Wilshire about it. A strange case." He stood. "But that's nothing you ladies have to worry about."

"We've worked out the sleeping arrangements," Doris said. "I asked Lieutenant Wilson next door if we could have the mattress from that single bed he isn't using. He carried it over and we've put it there at the end of the living room and Amy insists on sleeping there."

Colt shook his head. "Absolutely not. No guest in my quarters sleeps on the floor. You ladies take the bed and I'll be on the mattress. That's a much better place than where I've been sleeping the last dozen nights. No arguments. Amy sleeps in the big bed." He chuckled.

"Amy, I should warn you that Doris kicks and what's more she has cold feet, so you're fairly cautioned."

"Colonel Harding, I can't —"

Colt held up his hand stopping her. "Insubordination in my own quarters? I can't have that. And please call me Colt. Not another word." Colt looked at Doris. "Do we have any of that good cheddar cheese left and some of those crackers? That's what I missed most while on that ride with General Sheridan."

They sat around the kitchen table eating the cheese and crackers and talking. Colt quickly saw that Doris was drawing Amy out as much as she could, not letting her close up and keep everything inside.

"Bill and I only had the two kids. We wanted more and in time I guess we would. Oh my poor babies! They never even had a chance to grow up to live! But like you say, Doris, they're gone, just like your first family. Gone but not forgotten. So we can remember them with joy and not sadness."

"Yes, Amy. We have to be glad that we had that family and those loved ones for as long as we did. We can do that even though we're starting a new life, and moving forward again."

That night as Colt settled down on the mattress and pulled the blankets up over him, he marveled at how well Doris had handled the situation. Amy would come through this tragedy in good shape — mostly because Doris knew what to talk about and how to do it. The more he thought about it, the more he realized there was a lot he didn't understand about women, about how they thought, and how they acted and reacted to stress and pain, to joy and heartbreak. He grinned. He probably never would. Thank God he dealt mostly with men.

He rolled over, glad that he didn't have to deal with women and their emotions and curious way of thinking. If he did he'd be in lots of trouble rather quickly, he was sure.

Tomorrow. He had to dig into the second

murder tomorrow, but he was sure he'd find little that Doctor Wilshire hadn't told him. Now that case was a puzzler, a pair of puzzlers.

When morning came, Colt talked to Colonel Erhard about the Washita attack. There had been no new murder last night and Colt was glad about that, but he wished he was back at Camp Supply.

Before he left, he had heard General Sheridan planning:

"We're going to find Crawford and his men and with our expanded forces, drive all the way to Fort Cobb. We also need to find out what happened to Major Elliott. But I don't want you to go along this time, Harding. You get the wounded and Mrs. Whitright back to Fort Dodge, stay there and find out who that murderer is. I want that cleaned up as quickly as possible."

Then, General Sheridan had ordered scouts sent out on six different compass bearings to try to locate Colonel Crawford and his Kansas Nineteenth.

By nightfall the scouts were back. The easternmost team had found the Kansas troops still floundering around in the snow along the Cimarron River. They were given directions, told to rest the remainder of the day and strike out with first light. They were less than twenty miles away, but their horses were in terrible shape.

Back in Fort Dodge, Colt had pondered the murders most of the afternoon. The service records and talks with the men's Sergeants and Company Commanders had proved the same as before. The two men had no connection, neither was known to be a troublemaker.

The killer probably had only casual contact with the two men. So why were they murdered?

Colt tossed down his notes in disgust and pulled on his overcoat. He walked to the far end of the camp, past the paddock and the pasture where the cavalry horses huddled against the cold wind. The wind always blew in Kansas. It just depended how hard it blew and whether it was blowing dust, rain, snow or sleet.

At the far end of the fort he turned and walked back.

The chances were that the two men did not even know each other and that they died entirely by chance. Some unbalanced person on the post was playing out his own insane ideas of justice. He was venting his murderous anger on the men of Fort Dodge. Damnit, why?

Colt kept remembering the man in New York City that Dr. Wilshire had talked about.

The man was insanely furious because he lost one hand, so he did the same thing to others.

What anger could a soldier have that would make him kill and mutilate a man in that way. Some sexual anger? Frustration?

Colt stopped. The anger had appeared to be aimed at the men's sex organs. Could the man be a homosexual? Possible, but not likely. Such individuals were weeded out of the army quickly, not at all like the British army and navy.

So what did that leave him? Perhaps a man who had been abused by his father, even his mother? Colt's mind was reeling now. He was not trained for this type of work. He was not a doctor, surely not an expert on mental illnesses. Still, General Sheridan had ordered him to investigate. So by God he would dig into it until he solved the damned thing.

He turned and walked quickly back to the Fort Commander's office. Court martials. He was looking in the wrong area. The *victims* had not been court martialed, but how about the *killer?*

For three hours Colt scanned every major court martial during the past two years at Fort Dodge. He simply found nothing that he could imagine would trigger a soldier into a homicidal pair of torture killings like these.

Hate! There simply had to be a lot of

hatred behind this killer.

Colt talked with the doctor again.

"Yes, yes. I think your reasoning is good. The crimes both showed intense sexual anger and frustration. This hatred could have been held inside by the man for years. Now, I'll admit that in any army since the Romans, there is always a little homosexual activity. Ours is no exception, but it is muted and played down and minor. Any direct evidence, and both parties are summarily discharged.

"But you may be overlooking the other aspect — heterosexual activity. Normal sexual relationships or paid for sex."

"I've seen posts where the Commander has housed prostitutes on the base to service the men," Colt said. "Lots of times that led to tremendous problems. But we don't have that here."

"Colonel, you've been in the army long enough to know how our laundress system works."

"Of course. Some of the laundry women sell more than their laundry services. Some are pegged as 'officer' whores, and most go with the enlisted." He paused. "Doctor, are you suggesting that one of the laundresses may be involved here? All of these women are married . . . Oh, damn! It's possible."

"What's possible?"

"Say one of the laundry women is selling herself without her husband knowing it. The husband finds out, and systematically murders each man the woman services."

Dr. Wilshire lit his pipe and leaned back beside the stove in his quarters.

"Yes, yes, that sounds better than any idea we've had before. But many of these ladies are whoring every afternoon and evening. It's nearly a full time job. I don't see how they have time to do the cleaning and laundry. Why would only an occasional customer be whacked to pieces that way? With your logic, we should have fifteen or twenty killings a week."

"Maybe the angry husband doesn't find out about most of her whoring. Hell, I don't know. I have no answers, Doctor. If I was an expert on this psychology stuff, I'd be a high priced consultant in New York instead of freezing my ass off out here in the boonies. At least, Doc, I've got one more question to ask about these two men. . . ."

Colt went to the companies and barracks involved and talked to the men who slept on both sides of the two dead men. The talks were informal.

Colt used the first enlisted man's given name to make him more comfortable. Some of these newer troopers had never talked directly with an officer before.

"Wally, I know you knew Corporal Schultz. You were one of his good buddies. What I want to ask you now may help us find his killer. Will you help us?"

"Yes sir. I hate the bastard who done that to him, sir."

"Good. Wally, do you know if Corporal Schultz ever used the laundry whores?"

Wally looked away. He started to say something, then stopped.

"Wally, I know it's a hard question, but his death seems to be sexually related somehow. It's a question we need an answer to."

Wally looked back and sighed. "Not for a long time, sir. He used to get some once a month, like clockwork, but that was six, eight months ago. Then about a week before he got killed he told me he was gonna crack his nuts again, damn soon. He said he hadn't seen a naked woman for so long he was going crazy."

Colt felt a wave of excitement. "Yes, fine, Wally. We appreciate this. Now, did he say, or do you know, which woman he went to see?"

"No idea, sir. He once said the woman who did his laundry was a real pig, that he wouldn't touch her with a pitchfork. He thought she had some disease or something.

No sir, I don't know who he used."

The trooper frowned, turned away, then looked back.

"Come to think of it sir, I'm sure that he got himself murdered the same night that he told me he was gonna get some of the old poon tang. Said he had it all set up just after nine o'clock."

Colt tried to relax. "You're sure of this, Wally?"

"Absolutely. He even borrowed a dollar from me. Said the bitch used to be a dollar but she went up to two dollars, take it or leave it. He said he just had to have a good one or he'd explode."

Colt thanked the trooper and slipped out of the Sergeant's office where he had talked with three different men. When he worked the same questions for the last man killed, none of his friends could ever remember him going to a whore. One of the men was more specific.

"No sir, Colonel. He wasn't doing any whoring. He might have jerked it off now and then, but he didn't pay no juicy old whore."

One and one.

Colt was preoccupied at supper that night. Amy was teaching Doris how to knit. They had borrowed some knitting needles and the yarn from Captain Treadlow's wife. After supper, they huddled together and worked and laughed like a pair of school girls.

Colt stared at his notes. Whores. Damn them! That might be the case here. Both of the men *could* have visited the same whore. Both *could* have kept quiet about it. But why would a woman's husband suddenly fly into a homicidal rage and torture and kill two of his wife's paying customers?

Sleep, maybe that would help him sort it out and give him an answer. He was wondering how many laundry women were on the post, and how many of them sold their asses. It would have to wait until tomorrow.

Sometime later he woke and sensed someone near him.

"Took you long enough to wake up," Doris said softly, then slid under the blankets beside him.

He put his arms around her and kissed her seriously, then pulled away. "What if Amy wakes up?" he asked.

Doris laughed softly. "Just who do you think pushed me out of bed and told me to come out here and do my wifely duty?"

Doris was still on the living room mattress when Colt got up the next morning to build the fire.

"Good night's sleep?" he asked.

"It was just a terrific night!" Doris said. "I slept well, too." They both laughed softly so they wouldn't wake up the others.

Two hours later in the Fort Commander's office, Colt told the Colonel the ideas he and Dr. Wilshire had talked about.

"Mmmmmmm. Yes, it does seem possible. Of course, you know we have somewhere around thirty women on post who work as laundry ladies. All of them are married to enlisted men."

"That could cut our suspect list down from 300 to 30 husbands."

"If your theory is right."

"As of now, that's a damn big 'if,' Colonel."

"So what are you going to do?"

"Nothing right now we can do. We have to sit and wait, hope this maniac doesn't strike again, and if he does, that he makes a big mistake so we can grab him."

"Hell no! Don't grab the bastard. If you catch him in the act and you know damn well he's the one, shoot him down as he tries to escape. I don't want a long court martial on this."

Colt thought about it a moment, then nodded. "Agreed. Now all we have to do is catch him."

"How is your rescued lady coming along?"

"Just fine. Doris knew just what to say and what to do. I'd like to request passage for her on the next transport we send up to Fort Hays. She wants to go back to Ohio where she has some relatives."

"We'll have a sled going up in a couple of weeks if the snow continues. We'll put two light horses on a sled made from a wagon box and runners. I've used them before. A lot smoother ride than a wagon with wheels."

Colt nodded and stared out the window. He should be with General Sheridan at Camp Supply. But that was a hundred miles to the south. If he knew the General, he would probably have the troops on the march by now. It had taken Colt five days to get back to Fort Dodge. By now, Sheridan would be marching along the Washita. Colt wished he could be with them.

When General Sheridan and the troops arrived back at Camp Supply on December 2nd and found that Crawford and his Nineteenth still had not arrived, he sent out scouts in six directions and told them to follow their compass bearings. All scouts slanted northward from Camp Supply.

Late that day, one of the scouts returned with word he had located the wandering Colonel Crawford floundering around in the canyons full of snow on the Cimarron. Their horses were exhausted, some of them down.

Colonel Crawford said his troops would leave the next morning and arrive late the next day at Camp Supply.

With that settled, Sheridan and Custer went about resupplying their men, getting them ready for another run down the Washita. This time they would have more men and push any Indian force they found ahead of them or kill them in the process.

"Gonna wipe the Washita clean this time," General Sheridan said.

By the time Colonel Crawford's Kansas Nineteenth Volunteer Cavalry arrived in Camp Supply the next afternoon, most of the horses were ruined. Only six rode their mounts, the rest had been put down or could barely manage to walk to the camp under their own power without a rider.

The Nineteenth Cavalry had turned itself into infantry. It took another two days to refit the Kansas troops and get the men back on their feet.

Then on December 7, 1868, General Sheridan led the troops out of Camp Supply with nearly 1500 fighting men but with less than half of them mounted. Colonel Custer remained the field leader of the campaign.

The temperature was below zero when the troops left, each man in his blue overcoat. Some wore stocking caps and scarfs bound over their ears; others, regulation field hats. All had gloves now but no special snow boots.

Two days into the march a blizzard swept down from the north stalling their movement. On the fourth day they arrived at the Washita battlefield, and a detachment found the butchered bodies of Major Elliott and his fifteen men. Colonel Custer read the picture, saw that the men had been surprised, cut off, forced into the rocks and then cut down from behind.

The men were buried there and the march continued December 12. They followed a plain-to-read Indian trail that led down the Washita. They marched for five days and covered 76 miles, but found no Indian villages and no hostiles.

At Fort Cobb, General Hazen told Sheridan that since he had arrived there on November 8th, more than 6,000 Comanches, Kiowas and Kiowa-Apaches had come into the reserve to draw rations. They were spread downstream on the Washita and the Canadian for as far as a hundred miles. They were in the reserve they had been sent to.

Sheridan stewed and steamed. He was certain that many of the Indians now under Hazen's protection had been in the fight at Washita. But there was no brand to tell a friendly reserve Indian from a hostile. Sheridan and Custer and their 1500 men were angry and frustrated, but they could do little.

There were still hostiles to force onto the reservation, or to kill in the process. Lieutenant Colonel George C. Custer was determined to have it one way or the other.

Chapter Six

The next morning, Colt talked to the Fort Commander in his office.

"I need three enlisted men assigned to me for my investigation. One of them should be a Sergeant who can read and write and who is somewhat intelligent."

Colonel Erhard lit a cigar and grinned. He blew a perfect smoke ring at the beamed ceiling and growled. "Sounds like you're getting as frustrated as the rest of us around here about this damn killer. Fine, tell the First Sergeant what you need. If you want a place to work from, take the orderly room in what used to be J troop. It's open, and there's a stove."

The colonel knocked an ash off his cigar and stood. He cocked his head and stared at Colt. "You getting anywhere?"

"Not far. I still think the husband of one of the laundry whores holds the key. Right now I need to know how many of the sweethearts sell their asses and how many don't. I need to cut down the list."

By ten that morning, Colt had his three enlisted men and briefed them on exactly what he expected of them and what he wanted them to do.

"Everything said or done in this building and on this assignment is strictly confidential. I don't want you telling even your best buddy what's going on. If we're going to catch the son-of-a-bitch killer, we have to be as sneaky as he is."

Colt liked the Sergeant at once. He was about thirty, said he'd been in the army since he volunteered in the Civil War eight years ago. His name was John Flint. He was average size and had a sparkle in his eye Colt liked.

They sat around a table in the former Company Commander's office. Colt had out pencil and paper.

"First, I want to find out what you men know about the whores in the fort. How many of the laundry women sell ass?"

One of the privates snickered. Colt stared at him. "Trooper, this is not funny. Two men have been tortured and killed, and we think it might have something to do with the laundry whores and their husbands. So, the question still stands."

Sgt. Flint nodded. "I've been here two years now, sir. I've seen most of the women, heard about them, used a couple. I'd say that about half of them are active. Most of them don't really try and sell. They don't have to. They are there and if you ask, the ones that will, do it; and the ones who won't, throw a mop in your face. I'd say half sell their snatches."

One of the Privates guessed about the same number.

Colt wrote down 15 on his pad.

"Your first assignment is to find out for sure which of them are for sale right now, and which ones aren't. You'll probably have to simply go up and proposition them. I want their names and the husbands' names of each whore who is selling her butt. Divide the list however you want to. I want those names by four o'clock this afternoon. Now get out of here and get busy."

Sgt. Flint hesitated. "Sir, some of the women only sell it when their husband makes the arrangements, pimps for them."

"You know those names without asking the women. Put those down to start. Move."

Colt watched the men go out the door and turned back to his pad and paper and pencil. What else? What the hell else could he do to try to dig out this killer?

Peggy Fowler worked on the washboard in the laundry room. The big room was always the hottest in the fort — winter or summer. Hot water made for a hot room and for clean clothes, and that was her stock in trade. Two dollars a month for the enlisted, five dollars a month for the officers. She rubbed her hands to a red rash for the money, and it was hard earned.

Melvin had made her furious last night. He had said he had her lined up for five go-rounds in the next six days. He said at two dollars a pop, she was making more money that he was. He told her that just as he had her naked legs on his shoulders and was pounding hard to get his own satisfaction.

He never worried about her needs. Damn him! She had come close last night. He had rolled away and been sleeping within half a minute of getting serviced by her. She had slid out of her bed gently, hurried to the kitchen and brought back the sharpest butcher knife she had. She picked up his limp whang and put the sharp knife blade against it down by the roots.

For a full minute she left it there fighting with herself. Sure he'd bleed to death. Sure she'd have to stab him at least twice before he came fully awake. Yeah, she'd probably hang for her deed, but she wouldn't have to put up with his damned pimping any more.

Now back in the laundry room, she wrung

out the officer's shirt she had just washed, rinsed it in hot water and wrung it out, then rinsed it again in cold and hung it up. In wintertime the laundry ladies had to take turns in the laundry room because there was only so much space in the big building where they could hang clothes to dry.

Not that she minded a little sex on the side. Hell, she'd been rolling on her back and spreading her knees since she was fourteen, but now and then she'd like to pick the fucking man she rolled in the hay with!

She felt the urge burning in her. One more. Just one more and she'd be even with Melvin. Then she'd decide what to do about him. Who this time? He had to be somebody Melvin had not arranged for her to bed. Somebody she hadn't been with before.

Yeah! Peggy grinned and laughed softly. Right down from Lieutenant Paulson, who she cleaned for, a brand new Second Lieutenant had moved in. He'd only been on post for two weeks. He would be perfect. She finished the wash she had started, dried her hands, and made a stab at combing her hair.

Then she took her cleaning buckets and wandered down the row of officer country quarters. She tried the new officer's door but it was locked. She wasn't due to clean Lieutenant Paulson's rooms again for three days.

She moved down the row and killed time working on the windows of one of her clients.

A half hour later she saw her target walk down the row of quarters and go into his rooms. She finished the window and worked down his way.

She counted on the door not being locked. She tested it. Open. She unlatched the door and singing a little song backed into the room, dragging her two buckets with her.

She heard someone clear his throat behind her as she pushed the door shut. She turned around.

"Oh, pardon me Lieutenant Paulson, didn't know you was here." Then she saw it wasn't Paulson. Her acting job was good.

"You're not Lieutenant Paulson. What you doing in Lieutenant Paulson's quarters?"

He was about twenty-three, straight, tall, dark hair. A good looking boy.

He laughed. "No, I'm afraid you're the one who is mistaken. These are my quarters. As I remember, Lieutenant Paulson is next door."

"Oh, my," Peggy said. She had rigged her blouse before she came in and now reached into her blouse for a hankie. As she did, the cloth popped apart and one of her big breasts swung out. She pretended not to notice. She wiped her eyes.

"Sorry if I done upset you, sir. I better git."

"No, I mean not that way. You're quite exposed." He grinned but a blush began at his neck. "We can't have you wandering around half undressed that way, can we?"

Peggy looked down. "Oh, damn, got to sew on them buttons better. My boobies always getting through the fence." She paused, not making a move to cover herself. "I've got two, want to see the other one?"

"I have seen a woman's breasts before," he said but made no move to open the door for her.

"But not for a month or so, I'd wager," Peggy said. She pulled back her blouse so both breasts showed and walked toward him. "Hey, play with them a little. A girl likes to get her tits tickled now and then."

"No, really, I mean. . . ."

He hesitated. She caught one of his hands and pulled it up to her breasts.

"There now, feels good to me. How about to you?"

He laughed gently. "I am an admirer of fine breasts, and yours are top quality. Marvelous."

"I didn't want to clean any rooms anyway." She giggled. "Lieutenant, you do know what to do to make a girl get excited."

She reached for his crotch and touched him.

He pulled back for a moment. "What the hell, I'm free the rest of the afternoon." He bent and kissed both her breasts and she had three buttons open on his fly.

"Why don't we go in and see if the bed is made up," Lieutenant Ballard said. "That's a much better place for us to see what we can make out of this chance meeting."

An hour later, Lieutenant Roscoe T. Ballard was so drained, so exhausted, that he could barely lift his hand. He had just climaxed for the fourth time and rolled away on his back panting for air.

The inch-wide knife drove into his white belly so suddenly that he had no time to scream before Peggy's hand covered his mouth. He tried to get up but his belly hurt so bad he didn't want to move.

Then he saw the blade driving downward again and he tried to roll to the side but the knife beat him, plunging the second time into his lower abdomen, slicing through intestine and grazing a bone before it stopped.

"Bastard whore! What are you doing?"

"Teaching you a lesson, little boy. A lesson! Don't you ever tell me what to do again."

She grinned at him, showing one missing front tooth, then pulled the six-inch blade out sideways, cutting a three-inch path of destruction through his gut.

Lieutenant Ballard fainted. By the time he came back to consciousness, his torso dripped and ran with rich red blood. He looked at his body and screamed. Her hand was a little late but not much of the sound came out.

He tried to lunge off the bed, but got no further than up on his elbows when searing pain slammed through his system so brutally that he almost fainted again.

"What the hell?" he said coming to.

"Yes, Lieutenant, welcome to hell. You're going to have a good long stay here, so learn to enjoy it. I've been waiting for you to wake up. We're going to perform some surgery."

Peggy picked up his limp penis, stretched it out taut and made the first slicing cut.

Lt. Ballard screamed this time before her hand covered his mouth and just before he passed out again.

When he came back to the world of the near living, she had a cut-off piece of sheet around his mouth so he couldn't scream with any force.

She couldn't wait for him. Peggy used the knife again and again, slicing, cutting, chopping the officer's genitals until there was little left recognizable. He didn't come back to consciousness.

She stopped a minute and nodded. "Damn, these officers ain't no different than the pri-

111

vates when it comes to their privates," she said softly. Then she giggled. She dressed.

Peggy listened to the man's breathing. It was shallow, weak, his heart kept pumping blood out of his crotch and his chest.

Enough. She felt cleansed. She wiped the blood off her hands and arms onto one of the officer's towels. Then holding a towel near his throat, she slashed neatly with the knife and pressed the cloth in so the blood wouldn't spurt on her.

She wiped off the knife, slid it into her cleaning gear, went to the door and cracked it narrowly. It was snowing again, a real blizzard. She hadn't expected that. She saw no one along the officer's country walkway. It was just past five o'clock because the flag was down. She grabbed both of her cleaning buckets, stepped out the doorway and closed the panel behind her. Then she walked quickly across the parade ground with her head down to the laundry room and stowed her cleaning gear in her assigned spot.

She could wash one more batch. She shrugged, decided not to and said goodbye to the only other laundry woman there and walked to her small quarters out near the edge of the fort. The sudden snowstorm had passed. Peggy paused as she opened the door. Melvin would be there already and yelling at her about not having supper ready.

She snorted. She could take anything he could throw at her tonight. Peggy knew she had evened the score with Melvin for the next two or three weeks at least.

Colt Harding had returned to his quarters when he sent his three men out on their tasks. He could think of nothing productive to do, so he played with Daniel and listened while Sadie read to him from a McGuffey Reader one of the other officer's wives had loaned to her.

"You're learning to read as well as I can," Colt said. He tousled her blonde hair and remembered when she had been held captive by Walking White Eagle, the Comanche chief. So much had happened since those terrible days when the chief wanted to keep Sadie and raise her as a Comanche.

Doris came into the room, put another stick on the fire and sat down beside Colt. She kissed his forehead and put her arms around him.

"I've got to do this while I can. The army wives are telling me all sorts of little tricks to use to keep our men out of the field. Some of them work quite well. Right now I'm considering a false pregnancy. That always confuses the army doctors."

"You try that and I'll spank you," Colt said quickly.

"Not now," Doris whispered. "But please tonight."

Sadie went into the second bedroom to play with some rag dolls. Daniel was hard at work trying to whittle a fan from a piece of cedar. He had the notches cut. Next would come the delicate job of splitting the stick into the individual leaves of the fan.

"Wanda Erhard came right out and asked me today," Doris said. "She grinned at me and said she can do that because her husband is the Fort Commander. She said everyone was wondering about Sadie. She's so blonde and both of us are so dark headed. So I told her. She's such a nice person. She hugged me and we both cried a minute, and then she said she'd put a stop to any gossip on the post at once." Doris kissed Colt on the cheek.

"I really am a lucky lady," Doris said. "If it hadn't been for you, Daniel and I would both still be Comanches, living in tipis, eating buffalo jerky and pemmican, and running for our lives from the Pony Soldiers."

"So much has gone bad for the two of us, it's about time that something goes right," Colt said. He bounced her off his lap and stared into the fire. "Now if I can just find this killer, I'll be able to get back with the troops

114

and with General Sheridan where the important action is."

"No luck so far?"

For a moment he wondered if he could tell her. Then he knew he should. He told her everything he knew. She was a woman, she might have some ideas about this one. He put forth the theory he and Dr. Wilshire worked out about this being a sexually related crime. He expanded into his idea about the laundry women, and a furious husband.

"But you said these men know that their wives are prostitutes, some of them even help arrange for customers." Doris blushed. "I'm not comfortable talking about a subject like this."

"I know, but right now I need your feelings. Say one of these women's husbands didn't know what she was doing. Wouldn't that get him upset enough to want to go after the men his wife was entertaining?"

Doris laughed. "That's a man's question. You have to answer that one. Say I . . ." she giggled. "Say I was entertaining some handsome young officer, whether for money or not. Would you be jealous enough to cut him up that way and kill him?"

"Absolutely!"

"See, I said it was a man's question."

Colt pondered it a moment. He was getting

nowhere. "Let's put it this way. How would the woman feel, say, if her husband was pushing her into being a whore when she didn't exactly want to. What about her? How might the woman feel?"

Doris frowned. "I've never been in that position. I can only imagine how I might feel."

"Not quite the same. These women evidently don't mind whoring but they might not want their husbands telling them they have to."

"Oh, yes, that's different. So there would be resentment, anger. But I wouldn't think anything much more than that."

"Now let's play it the other way. You've never sold yourself, never even been sleeping with other men. Now suddenly I as your husband tell you I'm bringing home the Major and I want you to pop into bed with him. The Major is paying us ten dollars. How would a typical wife think?"

"Mad as all Billy hell. Furious. Fighting mad. But you're the husband. So . . . she'd have to do it, and start building up a hatred every time it happened."

"So much hatred that she might kill her husband?"

"At least — my God! Such a woman might be afraid to do that, but she would want to kill

116

one of the men her husband made her go to bed with."

"The innocent victim."

"Almost innocent, without him the woman wouldn't have been so angry, but mostly innocent."

Colt kissed her on the cheek. "Thanks, pretty lady. You've helped me. Now I have two kinds of killers to look for. It might be the husband of a part time whore he hadn't known about. Or it could be the woman herself who was being forced into prostitution. Now we're getting somewhere!"

Back at Colt's newly heated office, two of the men arrived by four o'clock. The third came in five minutes later.

When all of the men reported and all the notes and names were written down, Colt had a list of seventeen women who were active in prostitution on the base, all laundresses.

"Five of them right off the top we can say are run strickly by their husbands," Sergeant Flint said. "They don't even say hello to a man unless their husbands say they can. I've been around here long enough to know that."

"So we have seventeen suspects. Do these women use their own quarters?"

"Some do and some don't," Pvt. Plantain said. "They can always arrange a meeting in the supply room, or an empty barracks or even in the stables and tack room."

Colt looked at the list. "One more question. Are any of these women strictly for officers?"

Sgt. Flint nodded. "Yes sir. Four of them. They don't even touch an enlisted man. Those are the four at the bottom of the list since the men killed were both enlisted."

Colt thanked him and stared at the 13 names remaining. "Now comes the hard part. We have to start tracking these ladies. Most of them do their entertaining in the evening. I want each of you to put your initials beside one of the names from the top and do a scouting mission on them.

"Find a place where you can watch the woman's quarters, and write down when anyone goes into her quarters, or when she goes out to a meeting to lie on her back. Start right after you have your supper. Move now and get ready. Take your overcoats and a pocket watch if you can find one. Keep an accurate record."

The third name on the list was Peggy Fowler, wife of Pvt. Melvin Fowler. Sgt. Flint drew her name. He saw her go into her quarters just before five-thirty and she remained there all evening. No one went in or came out before midnight.

Lieutenant Ballard, being new on the post,

had drawn Officer of the Guard duty. When he was twenty minutes late reporting for duty at 5:30, the previous O.G. went to his quarters.

Ten minutes later a messenger jarred Colt away from his supper. A note from the Fort Commander told him to report at once to Lieutenant Ballard's quarters.

Colt, Dr. Wilshire and Colonel Erhard stared at the naked and mutilated body in a lake of blood on the officer's bed.

"Same butchering as the other two," Dr. Wilshire judged. "Only difference looks like a towel was used after cutting the carotid so the blood wouldn't spurt out."

"Goddamn!" Colonel Erhard said.

"Double that for me," Colt snapped. "I'm going to the quartermaster. He assigns cleaning and laundry people, right?"

Colonel Erhard nodded.

"Goddamn!" Colonel Erhard said again.

Chapter Seven

Colt found the quartermaster officer, Captain Casemore, in the officers' mess. He hadn't heard about the murder and hurried down to his office to show Colt the cleaning/laundry woman assignments.

The woman assigned to clean and do laundry for Lieutenant Ballard was Emmy Marsten. She was married to Cpl. Marsten. Colt got his quarters number and marched across the parade grounds.

Mrs. Marsten was about thirty and looked tired. She had two kids under five and a worried expression. She invited Colt inside and Cpl. Marsten was there in a second, saluting.

"Evening, Colonel. What can we do for you, sir?" Marsten was an old hand.

Colt did not explain why he was there. He started with a question. "Was your wife in or around Lieutenant Ballard's quarters this afternoon?"

Emmy Marsten shook her head. "No sir. I wasn't. He's scheduled for cleaning on Tuesday. This is Thursday so I was over at Colonel

120

Erhard's quarters doing the cleaning there. Mrs. Erhard and I been talking and working together from about one in the afternoon to well past six. She's getting ready for some kind of a party, I think."

"But you are assigned to Lieutenant Ballard, and no one else should be there cleaning?"

"Yes sir."

"Thank you, Mrs. Marsten. There's been a problem we're checking on, but it seems you could have had nothing to do with it. Sorry I disturbed you."

Cpl. Marsten opened the door and followed the officer outside.

"Is Lieutenant Ballard in trouble, sir?" Marsten asked.

"No, not at all, but someone else is, Corporal. Lieutenant Ballard has been found dead in his quarters. Thanks for your help."

Colt turned and walked away across the parade grounds and its frozen ground and half inch of stubborn icy snow.

By the time Colt got back to Ballard's quarters, his body had been taken away. Colt examined the three rooms critically. He lit all three lamps and put them in the same room and carried one, going over the place inch-by-inch.

After two hours he had found nothing out

of place, nothing that would give him any clue as to who the killer was. Not a boot mark, not a dropped hat or a scrap of paper. Not even the presence of antiseptic or soap from some just washed or cleaned area.

When it was nine o'clock, Colt gave up and went to talk to Colonel Erhard. The commander was in his quarters. He chewed, more than smoked the cigar he held.

"Anything?"

Colt told him about the cleaning woman and his frustrating search of the dead man's quarters.

"Figures. Goddamn! We have nothing. The same man must have done this one. Doc thinks so. We've got to stop him. This time he hit an officer. A fine young man who was well connected politically, which shouldn't mean a thing but we both know it does. He was the son-in-law of a United States Senator from Ohio. And there's gonna be pure wild-asses hell to pay for this. We've got to find the killer damn quick!"

"I'm working on an expanded theory now, Colonel. I know it's sexually motivated somehow. But now I'm thinking it could be either a man or a woman. Could be the husband of a whore who didn't know she was selling herself; or maybe the whore herself who isn't happy with her work; or with men; or with her husband who is forcing her into prostitution."

"Our laundry ladies?"

Colt told him about his list of the laundresses who actually were whores, and how he was putting a watch on them, three a night.

"So far, no results. This daytime kill doesn't do our theories any good, I admit."

"Tomorrow you get help, of a kind. I'm assigning First Lieutenant Rutherford P. Stanford to you. He's with Dog Company infantry.

"Lieutenant Stanford is a little hard to take sometimes. He's West Point, extremely bright, second in his class of '37, not at all bashful, and has done everything better than anyone else. But I think he'll help you. He'll report to your office first thing in the morning."

"Sound like punishment, Colonel."

"Not really. He's obnoxious sometimes, but has a sharp mind. He's red headed and freckle faced, but don't let that fool you any at all."

"I can't wait."

By the following morning, Colt had no more ideas how the investigation could be expanded or intensified.

He had just sent his three enlisted men out to watch the next three women on the list of selling-whores, when the new officer came in.

He doffed his hat, held it under his left arm and saluted smartly with his right hand according to regulations.

"Lieutenant Stanford reporting for duty as ordered, sir!"

Colt returned the salute and motioned to the chair. He reached out and shook hands.

"Stanford. Glad you're here. Colonel Erhard must have told you what I'm doing, our problem. I'm hoping that your fresh look at it might be helpful."

"A fresh look at a problem is usually productive, Colonel. As the poet said, 'Ah, the freshness of life, the stench of death.' We have a bit of both here."

"You've read the files, the reports on each of the killings?"

"Yes sir, I've seen all the reports you've given to the Fort Commander. I agree with the theory you and Doc came up with about the sexually motivated killings."

"Good. Did a man or a woman do it?"

"Sir?"

"Did a man or a woman kill the three men?"

"A man, of course. Brutal, animalistic, sadistic. And that one victim was over two hundred pounds. No, sir. Stake my balls on it being a man killer."

"So let's find him. I want you to talk to the

four women on post who are officer whores. You don't have to be quite that blunt about it, but interview them and see what you can find out. Especially look for one or two who feel that their husbands are forcing them into prostitution. If we can find just one like that, we may have a strong lead on our killer."

"Four? I only know of three."

Colt pushed a list over to him. "Four. I would suggest that you talk to them informally, either in their own quarters without their husbands there, or at their cleaning work place."

"Yes, I can handle that. Four, I'll be damned. I didn't know that I'd missed one!"

Both the men laughed.

"This Lieutenant Ballard, he was really politically connected?"

"Up to his armpits. His father is rich in Chicago, supports a lot of politicians and then there's always his father-in-law — the Senator in Washington D.C.

"General Sheridan will be hearing from him. You get going on those whores. I've got to see Doc Wilshire. Oh, you can use this area, or your own company office. I want to caution you, all we do here has to be extremely confidential. The enlisted men are close mouthed. You and I have to be the same if we're going to catch this bastard."

"I understand," Lt. Stanford said. He looked at the list. "Now there is a surprise, Willa. I didn't think she even banged her husband. Looks cold as a rock. Just never can tell about women, I guess."

Colt grinned. "Took me years to learn that."

A short time later in the medical offices, Colt leaned back in a chair and shook his head. "How in hell can somebody walk into officer country, kill a man, carve him up like a fatted calf, and walk away with no one seeing *anything?*"

"There was a bit of a snowstorm yesterday afternoon, you remember?"

"Yes, but don't we have interior guards? Is there no security here at all?"

"Damn little inside the fort area. Hell, Colt, usually we don't need it. We don't have Comanches or Cheyennes running around here."

"Same killer?"

"Yep. No question, same knife even. This killer is an extremely neat person. Always cleans off the knife on the dead man's clothes."

"Could a woman be doing it, realistically?"

"You bet. She gets the guy exhausted, he's relaxed, not expecting any trouble and wham, she stabs him where it hurts and he can't fight her. Even the two hundred pounder isn't going to fight if a knife slices through one of his testicles. Can you imagine how that would hurt?"

"I don't want to find out. Say, Doc, you have an inspection schedule for the whores?"

"Not as such. When I see them I suggest they come in for a checkup, especially when we get a big surge in the clap around here."

"I'd like you to check them all in the next two days. I've got a list, seventeen of them. Do the top thirteen first, then the four officer whores."

"Four? I thought there were only three."

"Four. Doc, you must have missed one. I had to test them all." They chuckled. "Use any excuse you want to. Contact them with a note delivered directly to them. I've got three men who can make the deliveries. They know the women in question."

"What's this going to prove?"

"I don't know. Pressure. The more pressure we can put on this killer, the better. Maybe he, or she, will make the big mistake and we'll have him right by the balls."

"Or by one tit," Doc said. "I'm leaning more and more to the idea it has to be a woman killer. Which means I'll be talking to her. Only wish to hell I knew which one it was."

127

That afternoon Colt talked to Lieutenant Stanford in the J troop little office.

"I've seen all four. I told them I was assigned to do an overview study on the cleaning and laundry operation, and wondered if they had any suggestions. All four of them were at ease and not flustered or nervous. They also had suggestions for the services, mostly that the army pay for the work and that they get higher wages. I said I'd put it all in my report."

"No help?"

"Afraid not, Colonel. One seemed a little hesitant, but I think she's new and a little afraid of an officer — at least while he has his clothes on. But she warmed up and wasn't nervous. In short, no help."

A messenger came in with an envelope for Colt. It had been through army mail and was water stained. He tore it open and read the usual scrawl of General Phil Sheridan.

"Colt . . . Got that murder wrapped up? I don't know what the hell Carr and Evans are doing. I want you to go up there and find them. They're supposed to be beaters, driving any hostiles down toward the Washita.

"Wrap up there in two days and bring us about twenty replacements for these troops. Leave there two days from whenever you get this. Say hello to Doris and the kids for me.

Looks like more and more of the hostiles are coming in to Hazen's olive branch. We'll see. It's a start.

"We'll see you when you get here. No firm schedule. We're in a slack period here for a while. Stop fooling around there with that little murder case and get your hindside down here. You'll go from here to Evans's base camp on the Canadian about 75 miles to the southwest."

It was signed Major General Philip Sheridan.

Colt snorted. "General Sheridan calls. You'll be holding down the investigation here. Sergeant Flint knows the other thrust of our work right now. They are shadowing the whores every night. Some of those women are really active. One of them had seven men one night."

"Hell, she's making more a month than I am," Lt. Stanford said.

When Colt told Doris about the new orders at supper, she gulped, put the kids down to bed early and told Amy she had to sleep on the living room mattress that night. Amy grinned and said it was about time. Then Doris led Colt by the hand into the bedroom.

"During the next two days and nights I'm going to wear you down to a small little nub," Doris said. She tried to do it all in one night.

The next morning, Colt cued in Lieutenant Stanford on the rest of the lines of investigation and told Colonel Erhard he had to go on a quick little mission for General Sheridan.

"Hell yes, pull you away just when you're getting close. Doc thinks things are winding down on the killer."

"All the programs are going ahead. You and Lieutenant Stanford can make the arrest as soon as you're sure. Or do you want to send a message back to Phil Sheridan saying you won't release me?"

Colonel Erhard bit his cigar in half and spit out the chewed end.

"Damn, just once I'd like to."

"But you like keeping those eagles of yours better. I understand."

The next day Amy was scheduled to ride a freight train of empty army wagons back to Fort Larned and then on to Fort Hays. At Fort Hays she could catch the Kansas Pacific Railroad and be on her way to Ohio. There were a lot of preparations. Doris made her a two meal lunch basket and the army provided rations as well.

Doris bundled Amy up in six layers of clothes including Doris's big buffalo robe coat Colt had made for her. There would be thirty freight wagons. The weather had turned clear and cold. The snow had melted down to a workable six to eight inches.

It was only a fifty mile run to Fort Larned. They would stay there a day and then move on another fifty miles to Fort Hays. Colt had arranged the layover for Amy's benefit.

They started at seven A.M. with four oxen pulling each empty wagon. Amy hugged both of them.

"I'll never forget you two, you both saved my life. I'm going to go back home and start over, find a nice man and make him a good home. I'm so glad that Colt found me that day on the Washita. If I have any more babies, I'll name them for you two, that's a promise."

The troops were getting impatient to be moving. There were bull whackers for each of the wagons and an escort of 16 well armed cavalry riders.

Colt and Doris watched the wagons go around the far building and north.

"There goes a lucky lady," Doris said. "Dressed the way she was in that tipi some trooper could have gunned her down thinking she was an Indian."

Colt caught Doris's hand and walked back to their quarters. "The lucky part came when you took over and put her mind back together. You made her into a vibrant, alive, interested-in-life woman again."

Doris kissed his cheek. As they went in the

door to their quarters she hugged him. "You really have to go? Why don't you get sick? You could be deathly ill from some strange disease. . . ."

Doris stopped and sighed.

"I know, you have to go. Tomorrow morning. You must go and there's nothing I can do about it."

"And nothing I can do either," Colt said. "When a General yells, a mere Colonel makes every effort to jump as high as the General orders."

Colt had a final meeting with his men. Sgt. Flint had a report.

"We've covered nine more of the women, Colonel. Only four left. So far we haven't seen anything unusual. Most of them have one customer a night, it all looks friendly and natural."

"What about the women who have husbands who pimp for them?" Colt asked.

"For them it's not so much fun," one of the privates said. "It's more like a job, for the money. I've seen a couple of them who were downright nasty to the men they screwed."

"Which ones, we should make special note of them and watch them again," Lieutenant Stanford said. Colt nodded.

"One was Erin Lassen and the other one was Peggy Fowler."

"All right. I want both of them watched. We've got a double cause to watch them now. Lieutenant Stanford will be in charge. Take your orders from him. If the detail winds down, keep watching the whores and in those last two cases, the husbands as well.

"Lieutenant Stanford, don't take any action against anyone without the consent and authorization of Colonel Erhard."

Colt watched them a moment. "We need to tie this up as fast as possible, but don't charge in without enough evidence. We need hard facts, firm evidence that will stand up in a court martial trial. Thanks, and I'll see you in two or three weeks."

Chapter Eight

Colt led the troops out of Fort Dodge and toward Camp Supply at a smart pace, covering a mile each twelve minutes. The five miles an hour pace was faster than most cavalry horses were used to, but they adapted well. He had twenty-two men, some of them recovered from their wounds and returning to their old troops and companies.

They made it to Camp Supply in the evening of the second day, hit no new snowstorms and could follow a fairly well trampled trail.

Colt had a hot meal and then reported to General Sheridan. The small man with the long arms and slightly large head stared at Colt from cold eyes. Colt knew he was thinking about something else.

Then he lifted his brows, nodded and shook hands with Colt. "Solved the puzzle yet, Harding?"

"No sir. Not yet. It's tied up somehow with the laundry women and their prostitution, but we haven't found the right combination."

"Damn them! I was on a post once where the Colonel brought in ten fancy ladies, put them in some unused quarters and set the price. They got medical attention, room and board, and a dollar a pop. Worked fine for two years. Then the Colonel's wife wrote a letter to Washington and old General Marshal himself stopped it.

"We never had any trouble with them, and the laundry women just washed clothes."

"Armies have had the same problem for centuries," Colt said. "We probably won't find the perfect solution. How are your beaters doing?"

General Sheridan moved to a wall map of the central plains. He pointed at Fort Bascom in New Mexico on the South Canadian River.

"Over here Major Andy 'Beans' Evans headed out a force of 563 men to sweep down the Canadian and explore the northern Texas panhandle and push any hostiles down toward the Washita.

"Evans has six troops of Third Cavalry, two companies of the Thirty-Seventh Infantry and four mountain howitzers. He moved his men out on November 18 up into Colorado and stopped at Fort Lyon on the Arkansas River.

"Up here Major Carr was to command a second column of his own Fifth Cavalry of seven troops and another four troops of the Tenth Cavalry and one of the Seventh. He had about 650 men. They were to move southward toward Antelope Hills at the head of the Red River. They left Fort Lyon on December 2, with my favorite young scout, a crackerjack named Buffalo Bill Cody.

"In the past, our scouts have told us there aren't many Indians in those areas but we need to sweep through there and see for sure. Both of the units are to stop along the South Canadian west of Antelope Hills and set up base camps."

"They should have them established by now," Colt said. "Maybe I can find them both there and get a report."

"Do that, Harding. Take six men as security and head out in the morning. Evans's base camp on the Canadian should be about twenty miles west of the Antelope Hills."

"Any special instructions for Evans, sir?"

"Just previous orders, sweep any hostiles south toward the Wichita mountains." He paused as if switching gears. "How are Doris and the kids?"

"Fine, sir. She's trying to turn me into a garrison soldier."

"All army wives try that sooner or later. That white woman you rescued on the Washita. How is she coming along?"

"Amy Whitright. She's just fine. We got her back to Dodge and Doris took over. She knew just what to do for her to make her feel like a human being again. The day before I left we put her on a train of empty supply wagons heading for the railroad at Fort Hays. She'll be going back to her people in Ohio."

"Good, good. Sometimes we get some small victories over these hostiles. Well, have a good trip. You might tag along with Evans when he moves down the Sweetwater and the north fork of the Red River. Could be interesting in there."

"Yes, sir."

Colt picked a Sergeant and he brought five privates with him for the detail with the Colonel. They left the following morning for the sixty mile ride to the Evans base camp. The trip turned out to be longer than that because they had to angle south toward the river and then follow it west to be sure not to miss the base camp.

They found it on the second day with no adventures. One of the privates, a long lean Texan named Maxwell A. Clark, who everyone called Mac, shot a big jackrabbit for their first night's hot supper. They roasted the animal over fires and each had a good portion.

When they arrived at the supply camp, Major Evans greeted Colt and made room for him in his Sibley tent.

"Old man checking up on me, I see," "Beans" Evans said.

Colt chuckled. "He wishes he had magic communication with every man in his command. He'd put a telegraph wire on every soldier and officer if he could so they could report exactly what they were doing."

"Better communications will come," Evans said. "Last summer we set up a heliograph between four outposts and the main fort at Bascom. We had instant notice of what was happening fifteen miles on each side of the fort. It was damn handy. So handy that some Apaches burned down one helio post and smashed the mirrors."

"I've used the helios, they really work. I heard somewhere that there's a man back in Boston who is trying to figure out how to talk through a wire. One just like a telegraph wire evidently, but the sound isn't dots and dashes, it's the human voice. He's probably a nut, but if it would work it would be great for a forward scout to be able to talk in a wire and for us to hear it back in the command post."

"Now you are talking crazy," Evans said. "Especially since tomorrow we start out on our run down toward the Wichita mountains. It's gonna be bust our butts all the way there and back through the snow, and I hope some Comanches."

"I'm going along. Do you really think we'll find any hostiles?"

"There are some Kiowas and Comanches out in there somewhere, but our scouts aren't sure where. We haven't found anything of importance yet. Just a lot of damn slogging across these damn frozen Texas plains."

Colt luxuriated sitting near the Sibley stove that had turned the inside of the round tent into a warm haven. He held out his hands near the sheet iron that glowed from the burning wood.

Colt looked up and waved at the stove. "Taking the Sibley with us tomorrow, or do we rough it?"

"Roughing it, except we'll take this tent along. Need to have one command tent. The other officers will have to do with shelter halves like the rest of the troops. Makes the officers a little more responsive to the needs of the men that way."

Major Evans rode out with 300 of his Third Cavalrymen the next morning and the rest of his men guarded the supply train and base camp on the south Canadian.

They made about twenty miles a day, poking into the smaller streams that wound into the South Canadian. Searching, they were always looking for a hidden pocket of hostiles who had settled in for the winter.

It was easy duty for a change. No hurry, beating clean a path along the Canadian, then cutting across country to the Sweetwater. They followed that down to where it dumped into the North Fork of the Red River. They were out of Texas now and back into Indian Territories.

There had been a break in the winter weather. It hadn't snowed since Colt arrived at the base camp. But that night the snow came down with a vengeance. It piled up eighteen inches before dawn and the men came out of their small pup tents wheezing and blowing on their hands.

Fires were authorized and warming fires sprang up all over the camp along the Red. Colt built one outside the Sibley and soon Major Evans came out to heat up as well.

"Damn snow will slow us down," Evans snorted.

"True, but it will give any hostiles camped along here the feeling that they're safe for the rest of the winter. They love to be snowed in, and safe."

"No Indian is safe anywhere, anymore," Major Evans said. "Not as long as Phil Sheridan is cracking the whip."

They still had the same troubles with the

light cavalry carts that mounted the mountain howitzers. They had four, and the carts often proved more trouble than good. They meant the troop had to take a different route at times to accommodate the one-horse pulled carts and the howitzers. Colt prayed that there was a chance to use the weapons after hauling them for a hundred miles through the wilds of Texas and Indian territories.

But the mountain cannon could come in handy. A good crew could throw out two twelve-pound shells a minute. With four guns firing it would be enough to send any Indian attack or campsite into a panic.

They worked down the North Fork of the Red River more cautiously. Evans put out two scouts riding a mile ahead of the main body. He also had two flankers out on each side of the men crashing along the ridges bordering the Red. He didn't want to be surprised. The flankers had such tough going that they were replaced every hour. Even so, the horses came back to the main line of march exhausted.

The North Fork of the Red River flowed due east for a while, then swung south. The next day a scout came back reporting he had seen horse tracks in the snow and what he thought was a three man hunting party far down the river.

Evans pulled his men to a stop and sent out

more scouts to determine exactly what was ahead. Colt went with the scouts and surprised them at his skill in tracking and evaluating tracks and activities.

They found where the hunting party had killed a large animal, probably a deer. It had been gutted and bled out, then probably cut into halves.

"Three unshod horses, three braves with winter moccasins. They used bow and arrows on the animal or we would have heard a shot." He sniffed. They were downwind of the Indians. There was no smoke in the air.

"We should move ahead cautiously. They had their horses so the main camp has to be at least five miles or more downstream."

Moving with great care, they covered the five miles, then they spotted two hunters on foot heading back along the banks of the Red.

"Sir, we better go back and report to the Major," the head scout for the group said.

"What can you report? Only that you saw some foot hunters. I'm going to move up on boot leather and see if I can locate the band's camp. It has to be close."

The scouts shrugged, made sure they had rounds in the chambers of their Spencer repeating rifles and followed Colt's lead.

They drifted from tree to tree, hung close to the ever growing larger Red, and soon found more signs of hunters. The wind shifted and Colt grinned.

"Smell that?" he asked. The youngest scout shook his head. The older civilian nodded.

"Smoke. Wind shifted. That village can't be more than a mile ahead."

They found it twenty minutes later and Colt began counting tipis spread along the Red. They were all on the other side, and fairly close together, but they couldn't risk counting them all. He got to 28 and stopped.

"Comanche?" Colt whispered to the lead scout.

"Can't tell," he said.

They pulled back carefully, watching both directions, and just as darkness fell, they slipped into the Cavalry camp past the posted guards who never saw them. As soon as the three were past two guards, Colt went back and chewed out the men.

"If we had been Comanches, you both would be dead by now and half the camp in jeopardy! Keep alert out here! Look alive or you might be looking at death before your time. Now sharpen up!"

In the Sibley tent, Colt reported to the Major. The veteran fighter nodded.

"We should be able to surprise the bastards. How far ahead, Colonel?"

"Five miles, maybe six. They're on the

other side of the river. We can keep our guns on this side and bombard them through an open space. I'd guess the camp runs for a quarter of a mile down the Red."

"Any lookouts, guards, sentries?"

"I didn't see any. If they were there and saw us, the camp won't be there in the morning. I'd suggest you send the scout back about midnight to check on the camp."

Major Evans grinned. "I don't mind taking advice from a Full Colonel, especially when he's right. If the camp stays there we'll be ready to move out by two A.M., be in place by five, and cannonade the hell out of that camp when dawn gives the gunners enough light."

"Major, do you know what day this is?"

Evans looked up curiously. "Nope, lost track."

"Merry Christmas, Major. This is Christmas Eve. We'll be attacking on Christmas morning."

Evans only nodded. "Yeah, Merry Christmas."

That was when Colt remembered what he'd heard about Bean Evans. A friend said that Evans had sworn a vow never to smile, and had lived up to his promise.

The troops got a few hours sleep. They moved out at three o'clock with blankets and overcoats. A half mile from the village, which was still in place, they stopped. They left their packs and overcoats there as they stripped for fighting. By four-thirty the four mountain howitzers were ready, spaced so they could each fire into a different quarter of the camp.

Major Evans didn't bother to surround the village. He intended to blow the camp apart with howitzer fire, then surge in and seize it before the Indians knew what happened.

Just before dawn three Indians were up, mounted their horses and rode out of the camp to the south. Major Evans told his men to let them go.

When dawn came, Major Evans lighted the first fuse and with that shot the cannonading began. Dozens of shells landed on the Comanche village of what turned out to be sixty lodges and became known as Soldier Springs.

The mountain howitzers did their job, shredding the camp, with the Indians left alive rushing away from the point of fire and leaving the village mostly to the south.

Evans moved his men into the camp quickly, routed the last ones alive and chased them downstream. At once Evans's men began burning the tipis and the food supply. Most of the horses had been run off to the south by the Indians and soon Evans found out why.

To the south lay a village of Kiowas, and

within an hour the Comanche warriors returned with reinforcements from the Kiowas. The Indians skirmished with the blue shirts burning their village.

Colt saw a dozen mounted warriors charging through a ravine directly at a weak spot in the blue coats line. He gathered a half dozen mounted cavalrymen and galloped directly at the weak point, meeting the Comanche and Kiowas head on. They soon were at pistol range and the cavalrymen loosed a murderous volley of rounds at the surprised Indians.

Four fell dead and three were wounded as they turned and galloped back into the brush and trees along the Red River. Colt's horse took an arrow in the neck but it wasn't serious.

Smoke billowed from the greasy pemmican and the pungent odor of burning buffalo jerky filled the air. Some men were detailed to mind the fires while the rest of the troops defended the village against the skirmishes.

The probes and small attacks by the Indians led Major Evans to believe that there were no more than 150 warriors on the attack. That would mean another village down the Red River of 90 tipis — but not a dozen camps that could produce a thousand warriors.

When the Kiowa and Comanche saw that

the village was a total loss, they pulled back. They had nothing left there to fight for.

Colt made sure that every stick and pot and utensil in the camp was broken, burned or ruined. He didn't want a single buffalo robe left for the Comanche.

Meanwhile, Major Evans took a report on the condition of his troops and horses. The horses were spent and a great many broken down. His force was in no condition to pursue the renegades. The cavalry had lost only one man. The enemy killed were estimated at thirty.

He let the Kiowas and Comanches go. His chances of catching them and beating them were too low to risk it. Major Evans turned his troops around and began a slow and painful retracing of his steps back toward his base camp well guarded on the South Canadian.

As they rode, Colt knew this was not a major battle in the fight against the Indians. But it did show that a cavalry force could attack in the winter and win. It put the Indians on notice once again that they had no safe haven in the winter, not even during a blizzard or behind three feet of snow.

A more evident result of the battle was the army's ability to destroy whole villages and the winter food supply for the tribe. Evans estimated he destroyed three tons of food that day.

The remnants of the two tribes moved on. Part of them went "to the blanket" under the protection of the army at Fort Cobb, not many miles west of the battle site on the other side of the Wichita mountains.

Many of them fought through the snow to the Kwahadi Comanche camp out on the Staked Plains in the Texas panhandle. The survivors quickly ran out of food and soon surrendered at Fort Bascom, Colorado. This was the same post from which Major Evans began his "beating in" exercise against the hostiles early in November.

Colt made it with his six troopers back to Camp Supply in time to check in with General Sheridan.

"Rest up here three or four days and then move up to Fort Dodge. Have a late Christmas with your family."

Sheridan's black eyes looked at Colt. "And get that damn murder case solved. It's getting to be an embarrassment. This officer who was butchered is bringing a flood of mail from important people. They want to know why and who. Clean it up!"

"I'll stick by it until I dig out the right person," Colt said. "Even if I have to personally test every laundry woman on the post."

Sheridan laughed. "You do that and Doris will be sure to kill you."

Colt found better weather as he and his force of six troopers headed out for Dodge. The first night it snowed, but they were deep in some brush and hardly felt it. The second day they pushed hard until they finally arrived at Fort Dodge.

When he clumped up to his quarters after dark, he saw a green paper Christmas wreath still on the door. He knocked, then walked in. Doris gasped with pleasure and held out her arms.

"Merry Christmas," she said.

Chapter Nine

Colonel Colt Harding scowled at the four men facing him in his temporary office.

"No progress? Nothing at all? What about those two whores who weren't happy? They been toeing the line?"

Sergeant Flint spoke up. "Sir, the word is out that all the whores are being watched. Right now their work is down about fifty percent. There just isn't as much sex being sold as there was two months ago. The women are being a lot more careful."

"So are the men and the officers," Lieutenant Stanford said. "The action is really down. Doc Wilshire says the cases of new clap are dropping as well. He did the physical examinations of the whores. Made three of them come in every day for medication and told them not to have sex with anyone, not even their husbands. He talked to the husbands of those three, as well."

"Damn! I was hoping we'd get a break. Evidently the killer is laying low along with everyone else. This was exactly what I didn't want to develop."

Lieutenant Stanford pushed a sheet of paper at Colt. "This happened last night. Probably nothing, but I figured you'd want to look into it. The perpetrator of the fight, a Corporal Tatterson, will be reporting here at ten A.M."

Colt studied the report from the Sergeant of the Guard. The man in question had beat up a private who had just taken a roll in the hay shed with the corporal's wife. Mrs. Tatterson was not on the list of women who sold their charms.

"Private Warnick nearly died from the beating," Lieutenant Stanford said. "Tatterson is a big man. He's up on charges. Warnick is in the fort medical ward."

Colt scanned the report. "This Tatterson will be here at ten, good. What about the two women we put a special watch on, the two who didn't seem happy in their chosen sideline?"

"Both of them have settled down, sir," Sergeant Flint said. "It could be because of all the pressure and the talk and tests and the three killings themselves."

"If I was the killer, I'd sure lay low for a while," Colt said. He stood and reached for his hat. The other men stood at once. "I'm going to go have a talk with this beaten man,

Warnick. If Tatterson gets here before I come back, wait for me before you start the interrogation."

In the medical ward in back of Doctor Wilshire's offices, Private Warnick sat up in bed. His jaw was taped almost shut. He would be on a liquid diet for three weeks to try to get his jaw to knit together. He couldn't talk very well so he used a pad and a pencil.

Warnick tried to salute but Colt stopped him.

"No saluting indoors, Private Warnick. Just relax, you're not the one in trouble."

"Good," Warnick wrote.

Colt chuckled. "I want to talk to you about the woman. What was her name?"

"Priscilla," Warnick wrote.

"You knew she was married?"

"Yes, sir."

"Did you pay her?"

"NO!" Warnick wrote.

"In the stables?"

"Yes, sir."

"Have you known her long?"

"Three months."

"Was this the first time?"

"No."

"So it had been going on for some time, a love match, and her husband just found out?"

"Yes . . . the bastard."

Colt watched the soldier tear off the filled up sheet on the pad of paper and look up at him. His face was bandaged except for one eye. One of his arms was broken. He had a broken rib and two more probably cracked from being kicked.

"The report said that Corporal Tatterson had a knife out and your pants down and was about ready to castrate you. Is that the way you remember it?"

"I was unconscious then."

"Had Mrs. Tatterson been in the hay with other men besides you here at the post?"

Warnick looked up and stared at Colt. Then he wrote. "Ab-so-lute-ly NOT!"

"Wasn't it risky bedding the wife of a Corporal who didn't know about it?"

"Yes."

"Was there a future for the two of you?"

"No. We lived life for this moment. Priscilla often said things like that. She's a poet."

Colt nodded. He shouldn't have asked. Again he watched the one eye in the sea of white bandages. Not much of a problem here. This case could have no connection to the three killings.

"Do you think Corporal Tatterson killed those three men here at the Fort?"

"No."

"Why?"

"He beat me up. He likes to use his fists and his boots. He's not a cutter."

"But he had out his knife."

"After he pounded me unconscious. The murders were done by someone angry, and good with a knife — all knife."

Colt thanked the soldier, told him to get well in time for the court martial, and went out to talk to the medic.

Doctor Wilshire had just amputated a soldier's leg who had been wounded on the Washita in November.

"Damn, I wanted to save it, but couldn't." He sat in a chair next to his desk and sighed. "You've been talking to Warnick?"

"Yes, at least *I* was talking."

"No connection to your murder case."

"You sure?"

"Yep. Sure as I am about anything these days. Tatterson is not a knife man. His method of operation is not the same. He isn't the killer, but that's just an old soldier's belly reaction."

"I agree. I'm back to where I was a month ago."

"I'm not. The clap is about half what it was a month ago. The whores are coming in for medical checks every month, and I told three more whores I was going to put steel chastity belts on them. They all have bad cases of the

154

clap. If I hear about them shacking up with anybody, their husband gets busted a grade and they get shipped out of the fort. It's working."

"Bully for you. That doesn't help me any."

"Puts more pressure on the killer. He'll make a mistake on the next kill."

"Another victim?"

"Maybe we can get him before he finishes the job."

"Maybe."

Colt said goodbye, arranged for an evening of playing the new card game, bridge, and went back to his office.

Corporal Tatterson was there, only he had been broken to private in a summary court martial by his Company Commander. He would lose his pay but not his food allowance for three months.

Colt and Lieutenant Stanford took him into the small office and they seated themselves while he remained standing at attention in front of them.

"Corporal Tatterson, did you kill those three men who were carved up like pieces of beef?"

"No, sir. Didn't even know them, sir."

"You did beat up Private Warnick."

"Yes, sir. He'd been with my woman, for three months she told me. I . . . I never laid a hand on my woman."

"Good, Tatterson, or I'd have done my best to get you hanged."

Colt looked at Lieutenant Stanford who shrugged.

"Tatterson, get out of here and report back to your First Sergeant. If you beat up anyone else as badly as you did Warnick, you'll be put away in a federal prison for ten years. Is that clear?"

"Yes, sir!"

"Dismissed!"

When he left, the two officers stared at each other.

"Right back where we started, sir," Stanford said.

"Nearly. Let's interview all five of the pimps on the base. I'm still leaning toward the idea they must be involved here somehow."

Stanford was on his feet moving toward the door. "I'll get the list and bring two of them in within half an hour."

"Go," Colt said and looked out the window.

It was snowing lightly again. Be three or four inches built up on the frozen ground by dark.

The first man in was Sergeant Gregor Daniels. He saluted and looked at the two officers. He was an old hand.

"Been in the army long, Sergeant?"

"Yes, sir. Twelve years. Fought with the Blue in the Civil War."

"How long have you been a pimp, Sergeant?"

"What? I mean, I don't understand, sir."

"You understand. You sell your wife's ass to enlisted men. No need to deny it. How long?"

Sergeant Daniels wilted. He began to sweat. His knees trembled. Lieutenant Stanford made notes on a pad of paper.

"For . . . for about three years, sir. We were short on money, and she said she didn't mind. . . ."

"You're sure she said that, soldier? Was she a whore when you married her?"

"No, 'course not."

"Then you made her one. Proud of yourself?"

Daniels took a long breath. He was so furious he could hardly talk. "No sir, not proud. We survived."

"You get up all of your wife's partners. Did she hold out on you and you found out and killed the men she slept with?"

"What? Hell no . . . sir. You talking about them three murders? Hell no! I'm no killer. I don't even have a knife. I'd use a revolver."

"Daniels, I'm thinking of starting a new rating. It's the rating of company pimp. You'll wear a pink vest over your uniform. The vest will have red lettering spelling PIMP on the back. How would you like to wear that all day, every day, Daniels?"

"I wouldn't . . . sir."

"Good. Think about it. Now get out of here!"

Daniels saluted, waited for Colt to return the salute. He didn't, and the Sergeant looked at the Lieutenant who shrugged. At last he marched out of the room and closed the door softly.

"A little rough on him, weren't you, sir?"

"I'm learning. All I have to do is get just one of them to crack and we may have a killer. Any better suggestions?"

"No, sir."

"Bring in the next one."

Colt used the same "bucket of cold water in the face" technique he'd learned when dealing with Rebel prisoners during the war. Hit them hard with a shock treatment and they lost their defenses and usually told the truth.

That morning Colt cross-examined three men including one whose wife the reports claimed had been on the mean and nasty side with her customers.

That one was Melvin Fowler. Colt got little but surprise and anger from Fowler.

When they were done with the five men in the middle of the afternoon, Colt and Stanford went back over them.

"Fowler was the coldest son-of-a-bitch I've ever talked to," Lieutenant Stanford said. "It was like he was an animal, or a machine, with no feelings. Sure he pimped for her pussy, he said. She didn't mind, why should he? It doubled his income as a soldier. No army officer had ever objected before."

"Patterson was the other side. He was sympathetic. But he said they had to have the extra money. He was the one who said he would rather stop his wife whoring than get out of the army. I remember that."

They both looked at the notes.

"So, Lieutenant. Where are we now. Did you pick the killer out of those five men?"

"No, sir. They were pimps. If their wife had been getting extra work they didn't know about, they wouldn't kill off a good customer. They'd simply slap their wives around a little and demand that they turn over the money to them and let them set the prices the next time. None of these men were stupid enough to kill the customer."

"Damn!" Colt thundered. He threw down his pencil and looked outside at the Kansas snowfall. "That's about the same line of reasoning I came up with. Another damn blind alley, a box canyon we're thrashing around in. How in hell do we get out?"

Colt went to the door and called in the three enlisted men. He briefed them about what the officers had just learned from the pimps.

"Now, you men know what we know. You've been in on this from the start. Do any of you have any ideas what we might do next to find this damned killer?"

Sergeant Flint looked up. "Sir?"

"Flint?"

"My father is a medical doctor in Chicago. He works with the police there a lot trying to figure out why killers go on angry bloody rampages. He's trying to dig into people's backgrounds and their minds and find out why they're so angry, and maybe be able to stop some of the ones teetering on the edge. He's done it a time or two.

"That's why I was so interested in this problem. I was trying to look at it the way he would. We've got a limited number of suspects. You say the five pimps probably aren't good suspects anymore. That cuts it down to the whores themselves.

"I'm probably wrong, sir, but I think you should talk to the whores the same tough, angry, demanding way that you did with the pimps. One might break down and confess."

Lieutenant Stanford looked at Flint with disdain. "Sgt. Flint, you're not the doctor here. How can you say we have only those 23 whores, or 17, or however many it is, as suspects? How could a hundred pound woman kill a two hundred pound man?"

Sgt. Flint sat perfectly straight in the chair near the desk.

"Sir, all of the victims were naked. It's my suggestion that all had been thoroughly worn out through sexual intercourse, two, three, four times. Then when the victim was trying to recover from his last 'mini death,' the whore could easily stab him once or twice in some vital area that would incapacitate him.

"Those stab wounds in the belly would hurt a man so much he wouldn't even be able to sit up, let alone turn over or get up and walk. Once the man was at her mercy, she could cut him up any way she wanted to, slicing up his genitals and then killing him just before he bled to death."

Colt grinned as he sat back and looked at Lieutenant Stanford.

"Your rebuttal in this debate, Lieutenant," Colt said quietly.

Lieutenant Stanford looked up and shrugged. "Yes, Sergeant, your logic is good. I can't argue with it. Since we've about cut out the five pimps as suspects, you're right.

161

Our best suspects remaining are the whores themselves."

"Flint, you've talked with more of them than any of us. Who would you suggest we should bring before our inquisition first? Pick out five."

"Well, I still have an uneasy feeling about those two we found were angry . . . Erin Lasser and Peggy Fowler. Then I can come up with three more. The ones who love the work don't seem like they would be candidates."

Colt went to the window and watched the snow. He turned and found a long thin cigar he'd been saving. He lit it and let them wait. Then he nodded.

"Okay, Sergeant Flint. Go round up this Erin Lasser and bring her back. We don't have a damn thing else to do, so let's talk to her. One suggestion. I want my wife to sit in on these talks. She's not a prude, but she knows a lot more about how a woman thinks than any of us men.

"You go find Erin, Sergeant Flint. I'll go see if I can talk my wife into helping us."

It was just after four-thirty that afternoon when Colt came back to the J Troop orderly room with his wife.

Doris hesitated just inside. "This is going to embarrass the woman, Colt. She might not say a word when she sees me."

"Maybe, but I don't think so. These women are not the kind who will get embarrassed easily. They are prostitutes. How can they be unhappy talking about it?"

"Just a feeling I have."

Colt laughed. "That's exactly why I want you along, to get a woman's feeling about each of these whores."

"What if I see them on the post?"

"They won't be coming to the officer dances, if that's what you're thinking. Now let's give it a try."

They went into the inner office and Lieutenant Stanford and Sergeant Flint were there pouring a cup of coffee for Erin Lasser.

"Here they are now," Lieutenant Stanford said.

"Sit down and let's get started," Colt said coldly. "We're not here for a social chat." He had remained standing and stared hard at Erin. She was Irish, cute as a lady bug on a picnic basket and she smiled up at him. She was also slender and full busted.

"Erin, why the hell are you a whore?"

Her smile never flickered.

"Because I can make more money than my husband, and it isn't hard work, and I rather enjoy the attention. I'm good at my work and I'm a popular lady on this post."

"I've had reports that you get nasty and talk with a foul mouth with some of your customers," Colt said.

Erin laughed. "I don't know where you heard that. But I admit that I don't like the way some of these assholes smell. Then when I get the curse, I always get real nasty. Happens once a month like clockwork. The bastards could at least have a bath before they want to jump in bed with me."

"How long have you been selling your body, Erin?" Lieutenant Stanford asked.

"Long before you arrived. Yeah, I service the enlisted. Ain't fancy enough to fuck you officers." She turned to Doris. "Honey, I don't know why you're here, but I do talk a little like a mule skinner sometimes. Don't be embarrassed."

"You said you enjoy servicing these men. Is that true?" Colt asked that question.

"Usually. Sometimes a guy will get rough. Then I take out my little .45 over-and-under derringer and make him leave. I don't put up with any rough stuff. I mean, a girl has to protect herself, right?"

"I thought you preferred a knife?" Sergeant Flint said.

She looked at him. "Well, glory, the Sergeant here can speak after all. No, honey, I don't use a knife. Hate knives. I don't get a rotten John very often but when one gets rough or I know he has the clap, I pull out the derringer and tell him to get his pants on and leave, and so far they always have."

"Have you ever shot one of your customers, Erin?" Colt asked.

"Naw . . . hey, what is this? You saying I killed somebody. . . ." She jumped up. "Lord Almighty! You think I had something to do with butchering up them three men — that officer and them two enlisted. That's a bunch of shit! I never even knew them guys. The officer for damn sure. I might . . . I mean, in five years I seen lots of guys. Yeah, I might have cracked the balls on one of them sometime back aways. But I don't remember the names.

"Hell, I didn't kill them if that's what this is all about. Why should I? Kill the goose that spits out the dollar bills all the time? You're the ones who are crazy if you think that way."

She stood. "Well, do you nice people have any more questions? How about you, ma'am? You have some crazy question for me?"

Doris frowned, then nodded. "Yes, I do. How did you ever get started . . . doing this?"

"Whoring? You can use the word. Good word. Damn, been so long ago I near forgot." She laughed. "Not really. I had this uncle who was a character. He liked young girls, and he got me in the hay on our farm when I was thir-

165

teen. I liked it. I mean I guess some women don't, but I did, from the very first.

"He came to the farm often, and one week I stayed at his place in town while my folks went to bury somebody. He and me went wild for three days — about six times a day." She laughed. "He was worn out. He said he had a good friend he wanted me to meet, and asked if it was all right. I said sure, as long as he didn't tell my Pa who would half kill me.

"So he brought his friend and he wanted what my uncle wanted, but when he left that night he gave me a dollar gold piece. A whole dollar! I was fourteen by then. The next friend who my Uncle Lou brought the next night I told it would be a dollar and he dug it out fast and quick before I even got undressed.

"So, nice lady with the Colonel, I guess that's how I got started whoring."

Sergeant Flint and Lieutenant Stanford had both been writing on their pads.

Colt stood. "Mrs. Lasser, I guess that's all the questions we have for you. One thing more. You're a good talker. But if I hear that you've said one word to anyone about this meeting, or what we talked about, or who was here, I'll have you declared an unfit person to be at the fort and get you shipped out of here so fast you'll forget your corset. Is that perfectly clear?"

"Sure is, honey. I know when to shut my yap."

Colt led her to the door and she went out into the still gently falling Kansan winter snow.

Chapter Ten

Colonel Harding came back to the desk as soon as Erin Lasser left the office and looked at the four men and his wife.

"She couldn't be the killer," Lieutenant Stanford said. "Not unless she's a terrific actress. She enjoys the work too much."

They looked at Doris Harding. She cleared her throat. "She is the first — the only woman — I've ever met who is in that line of work. She seemed absolutely sincere. I don't believe that she killed the three men, or that she could. She might shoot somebody if she was frightened enough, but she couldn't use a knife."

Colt lifted his hands. "So we'll talk to the other woman tomorrow. Nine o'clock, right here."

The three enlisted men stood and left the room.

Lieutenant Stanford shook his head. "That woman was something, a real strange character. But not a killer. Well, Mrs. Harding, Colonel, I'll see you tomorrow."

At home that evening they talked about the

events of that afternoon. Colt agreed with Doris that Erin Lasser was one of a kind.

"How she could do that and then talk about it that way . . . I just don't understand that kind of a woman."

"Good!" Colt said.

Colt and Doris and the two kids played dominoes until time for the young ones to go to bed. Playing dominoes was how Colt first learned his numbers. Daniel and Sadie were coming along fine. They could do their fives-times well to score points. But adding up the numbers to get there was still a tougher task for them. There was no hurry, they would learn.

The snow stopped during the night. Eighteen inches of a brilliant white frosting covered the fort. The sun was up early that morning turning the pupils of anyone's eyes who was outside into tiny pin points that still let in too much light.

Colt and Doris trampled across the snow that morning. The kids both went to a neighbor, a Captain Libera who also had two children about the same age.

"Who do we talk to this morning?" Doris asked.

"Peggy Fowler. I spoke with her husband a couple of days ago. He seemed cold and uncaring, but not the murdering type. If we check out these five and have nothing, I just might ask for a transfer to San Francisco."

Doris smiled at him, knowing he wouldn't, but also feeling his frustration.

Everyone was in the company orderly room waiting when Doris and Colt arrived. He introduced Doris to Peggy and they went into the office and sat around the room. Sergeant Flint had made coffee and got the fire going so both rooms were warm today.

Peggy Fowler was in her twenties, plump without being fat and did not dress to conceal her generous breasts. Her blonde hair had been washed recently and even combed where it hung below her shoulders. Her face had a few small pitted scars and Colt judged her at once not to be pretty. Her hands were clean from her scrubbing work and nails broken. She wore a simple print dress that swept the floor. Before long she took off a plain heavy coat and put it over the back of her straight chair.

Colt began it. "Mrs. Fowler, do you know why you were called in here this morning?"

"No, sir."

She was army enough to answer with a "sir."

"Good. You're listed as a cleaning/laundry worker, paid by those you work for. Is that correct?"

"Yes, sir."

"But you also perform certain other services for the enlisted men of the post that your husband arranges for you. You're a working prostitute. Is that correct?"

"Yes, sir."

"Are you a whore because you want to be, or because your husband has forced you into it?"

Peggy looked up, her eyes going wide for a moment, then she frowned. "Never thought much about it. Started five, six years ago when he was a Corporal and we was always short of money. Guess I agreed back then. Wasn't too bad. For a while I even enjoyed making those men happy."

"For a while, you said. Do you enjoy it now?"

"Hell, no." Peggy looked at Doris. She made a motion with her hand. "Hell, Mrs. Colonel, you know how it is. At first fucking is all romance and new and strange and then it gets to be interesting and fun and for a few years a bride enjoys getting poked by a man she loves.

"Then, it gets different. Just servicing a husband is a real hard job after a few years. You're young, just wait, happens to every wife. Then when you have to start spreading your legs for strangers you've never even seen before . . . that is harder yet."

Peggy was talking to Doris now, she barely heard the others. Lieutenant Stanford asked her a question, but Peggy didn't respond. Doris repeated it to the woman.

"Peggy, does your husband set up each time for you, makes the contact with the man and gets paid?" Doris asked.

"Oh, for damn sure! He handles the money. Some girls can flutter their eyelashes and make dates to get poked, but I never was much good at that. So Melvin takes care of that. We make more money that way."

"Does your husband drink up the money, or does he gamble with it?" Doris asked, aware that now she was the only questioner Peggy would talk to.

"Yeah, both, and he does some whoring, too. I don't care. Long as we have enough for rations and a dress now and then from the catalog."

"Was your husband the first man you made love with?" Doris asked.

Peggy laughed. She threw her head back and screeched with glee. Tears came to her eyes. She brushed them away, got control of herself and stared at Doris.

"Your husband was first for you, I can tell. Hell no, not for me. When I was little, we lived outside of Chicago, and my mom ran off with somebody when I was five.

"Me and my brother was left at home, so Dad had to take care of us and work too. He come home tired and had to give us our baths. I guess I was four. He liked the baths because he could look at me naked and wash me and poke around.

"We played sex games when I was six and he let me play with his big prick. I didn't know no different. I thought all little girls did that with their dads.

"When I was ten he was dry fucking me between my closed up legs and I was eleven when he raped me the first time. I found out from the girls at school that nobody had ever even touched them and I told my dad it was wrong and he laughed and did it again. Once a week was all right, he said.

"When I was twelve I ran away to my aunt's house and told her about it. She put me in the basement and hid me from my daddy and I never saw him again.

"The older boys found out about it, and when I was fourteen they made me do it again. So I ran away. A woman found me in an alley and invited me to her house. She was a madam and I became a full time prostitute when I was fourteen."

Doris had been nodding and listening. Sergeant Flint wrote hard and fast on his yellow notepad.

173

"Do you hate all men, Peggy?" Doris asked.

She sighed. "Hell, maybe I do. Sometimes I want to tell Melvin, no more. Tried that once and he hit me so hard I was unconscious. Ain't gonna try it again."

"Some of the girls carry a derringer for protection. Do you carry a derringer, Peggy?"

"Land sakes no! I'm afraid of them firearms. People get kilt with them all the time."

"Have you ever thought of killing Melvin to be free again?" Doris asked softly.

"Sure. Lots of times. When he's hitting me. Damn. I hate him then. But he don't hit much. I'm living. I ain't in a regular whore house. Good as I can get, I reckon."

"Peggy, have you ever hurt a man you had been with, you know, afterwards when he was recovering?"

"No, but that'd be the time to do it, wouldn't it? Them panting and wheezing like a railroad steam engine. Yeah, that'd be the time to shoot the bastards."

"But you never have?"

"Afraid of guns, never do carry one."

"You've heard about the three men killed here at Fort Dodge in the last month or two?"

"Yes, heard about them."

"Do you think a woman could have done them all?"

"A woman? a whore?" she shrugged.

"Yeah, I guess, if she was mad enough. If the guy hurt her or something. Could'a."

"Peggy, have you ever hurt one of the men you've been with?" Doris asked gently.

"Oh, Lordy, that again. Yeah, I did about two years ago. I got all excited and bit this Sergeant on the neck. He even bled. I took quite a teasing about that. Ain't happened since, I tell you true."

Doris looked at Colt who nodded and pointed at the door.

"Thank you, Peggy. I think that's all the questions we have for you. You can go back to your quarters now."

Peggy looked at Doris. "You're a nice lady. Thanks for acting fine to me. The other officers' ladies treat me like a whore. One spit on me once. Couldn't figure her out. A high and mighty Second Lieutenant's woman."

Peggy stood, and the men around the table came to their feet automatically. She smiled at Doris, and walked out of the office.

They all had opinions. It was close enough to noon that Colt and Doris walked back to their quarters.

"You didn't say what you thought about Peggy," Colt said.

"I haven't decided. Mistreated by her father from six and raped at eleven and a runaway at twelve!" Doris shivered. "That's so terrible, monstrous. I wanted to put my arms around her and tell her it wasn't her fault. Whatever she is today is the responsibility of her father. I wish we could hang *him!*"

Colt looked at her in surprise. He'd never heard Doris say anything quite so sharp, with such anger.

"She said she never carried a gun," Colt pointed out.

"Yes, but she didn't say anything about a knife. I'm still going back and forth. She certainly has enough reasons to hate every man she sees. A prostitute when she's fourteen and then forced back into the business when she marries into the army. I just don't know."

"We wouldn't have learned a thing without you there today. Did you realize that she talked only with you? It was as if the rest of us weren't there."

"Poor soul. So pathetic. So angry."

"Is she angry enough to kill, to torture a man that way?" Colt asked.

"I'll need some time to think it through, a day or so at least. Let's not talk to any of the other women today."

"We won't."

They came toward their quarters and Doris giggled. "Look, it's Kirk waiting for us."

"Who?"

"Kirk Rossman, the young man I told you

176

about. He's sixteen and he has a crush on me."

"I remember, two months now. You've been encouraging him."

"Not a bit. I just act natural. His mother is visiting back east for the winter. I think he misses her."

"Not a chance, he's sixteen and horny and has a crush on you. You handle him, I'll go get the kids."

When Colt got back with Sadie and Dan, Kirk was shoveling off the walkway in front of the quarters. He waved at Colt. Inside Doris laughed.

"I told him not to do it, that it would melt or blow away, but he insisted."

"No harm, make some hot cocoa for him." Colt peered out the window. "He's small for his age, you say sixteen?"

"Almost sixteen, birthday . . . oh, Lord, tomorrow! And his mother gone. I've got to ask his father if we can have a birthday party for him. Sixteen, an important time."

"Kirk's an only child?"

"Yes, and he has no self confidence at all. I wish there was something we could do."

"Can he ride a horse?"

"His father is cavalry, of course he can ride."

"Good, I'll teach him something this afternoon to boost his self confidence. First I find his father and clear a party for tomorrow. Evening?"

"At sixteen, yes, evening. I'll try to find out how many children in their teens there are on the post."

When Kirk came in after shoveling the snow, Colt insisted that he accept a quarter for his labors. They sat around the kitchen table talking and sipping cocoa and coffee.

"What are you going to do when you grow up, Kirk?" Colt asked.

"Cavalry, just like my father. First I'll need to go to West Point, but he says he thinks he can get me in a class."

"Can you ride?"

"Sure. I ride all the time in the summer. I get a mount and go tearing around."

"Want to ride this afternoon?"

"In the snow?"

"Sure. A cavalryman has to be able to ride in all kinds of weather. I'll show you a riding trick if you'd like."

"Hey, sure! What time?"

"Meet you at two o'clock at the stables."

"Fine! Fine. I'll be there." Kirk finished his cocoa, looked at Doris with a big smile and hurried out the door.

After the midday meal, Colt told his men their star interrogator couldn't work that afternoon. "She's still thinking over what we heard from Peggy Fowler. We'll go with three more first thing in the morning."

He found Captain Rossman. He was a career soldier who had been a Brevet Bird Colonel at the end of the Civil War. He was reduced to First Lieutenant and was back up to Captain, his best permanent rank. He was delighted with Colt's offer to give Kirk a birthday party.

"He said he liked to ride. I thought I might give him a lesson on riding Comanche style this afternoon, if it's all right with you?"

Captain Rossman smiled. "You bet. I don't get to spend enough time with the boy, and with Martha gone back east . . . well, he's been a handful. One of the women complained that he was hanging around her quarters all day. I got him straightened out on that."

"We'll have the party tomorrow night at seven so the kids can be home early. Doris is rounding up all the kids in their teens. I don't know how many that'll be."

Promptly at two o'clock, Colt had two army mounts at the paddock gate all saddled and ready. Kirk ran up and saluted and Colt returned his salute.

"Cadet Rossman, reporting for duty, sir!" Kirk said.

"Mount up soldier, let's ride."

They walked their mounts to the parade grounds, where some of the cavalry units still on post had done their daily drill. Now the area was deserted. It had been trampled down so there was good footing. They stopped.

"Kirk, one of the problems in Indian fighting is when a warrior will swing off to the side of the horse and ride past you. You can see only one foot and maybe part of his leg. Then he shoots under the horse's neck at you. You don't have a target except the horse.

"I've trained special companies to ride the same way. Would you want to try it?"

Kirk's eyes were wide. "Anybody on the post know how?"

"Probably nobody except me. Let me show you what I mean." Colt slid out of the saddle to the right, brought his left stirrup up with his left foot and hooked his toe in it upside down. Now he slid more and more off to the right side of the horse until he was nearly out of sight behind the animal. He left the reins loose on the horse's mane and with his left hand grabbed a handful of mane to support himself.

He drew his issue revolver and pretended to fire under the horse's neck as he leaned solidly against the horse's chest over its right leg.

A moment later he hoisted himself back in the saddle.

"That's all there is to it, Kirk. Now watch while I do it when I'm moving." He rode away from the boy fifty yards, then turned and came back. He slipped off on the right side again and pretended to fire under the horse's neck again. He angled to the left so Kirk could see how he was positioned, then did a circle around the boy and pulled back into the saddle.

"Jumping jackrabbits!" Kirk breathed. "Never seen anything like that before!"

"Think you can do it?"

"Golly, gee gosh! I don't know. Can I try?"

Colt helped him as he brought up his left stirrup and put his boot toe in it.

"Now start sliding off the horse on the right side. Go slow. That's it. Grab that left hand full of mane and lean down some more."

Kirk looked at Colt under the horse's neck.

"Now, pretend to fire. Just getting away's no good, you have to fight Indians that way."

Colt made Kirk do it five times by himself, then told him to get in the saddle.

"Now we do it moving, with your mount at a walk." Colt took the reins so the horse would keep moving and Kirk slid off, hooked his boot in the stirrup and promptly fell off the mount into the snow.

"Forgot my left hand on the mane," Kirk said. The next time they did it walking, Kirk did it perfectly. They did it twice more, then Colt mounted up.

"Now, we do it at a canter. Not much different. Remember each step."

Kirk made it the first try and whooped like an Indian and rode faster toward a pair of troopers walking across the parade ground. He whooped and yelled at them and they ducked as he rode by pretending to shoot them. They stopped, amazed, puzzled. When he turned and rode back to Colt he was grinning, his face split open and teeth glistening.

"How was that?"

"Fine," Colt said. "See that infantry company down there drilling? Let's attack them. Both of us on this side hanging off. Next you have to learn to do it on the left side, but it's almost the same."

"Let's go!" Kirk yelled.

They cantered toward the infantry company with a Sergeant putting them through a drill. When they were thirty yards away they dropped down on the right hand side of the horses and streaked past the troopers at ten yards firing their fingers for revolvers.

The troops stopped the drill and stared. Colt and Kirk turned and rode back on the far side again hanging on the right in the simulated attack. The troopers saw nothing more than a boot on the saddle and a face firing a finger under the horse's neck.

Colt and Kirk lifted back into their saddles and rode off toward the stables.

"Those guys will have something to talk about tonight!" Kirk said. "Tomorrow I'm going to practice some more so I can do it faster. I've got a cartridge belt and a .32 revolver. I'll try it with the weapon — unloaded, of course. Then I have to learn to ride it from the left side."

"Show your dad tomorrow, I think he'd be interested. Maybe you can be the instructor to teach his troop that maneuver."

Kirk was wide eyed again. "Wow, wheepers! You think so? First I'll get real good at it, the way you are."

They rode back to the paddock and turned the horses over to a stable man.

By the time Colt got back to his quarters that evening, Doris had discovered six teens on the post and promptly invited them to a birthday party. She had written invitations delivered to all them before supper time.

"How did the riding lesson go?" Doris asked.

"Better than I expected. Kirk caught on quickly. I'm going to ask his father if he can teach volunteers from his cavalry troop the maneuver. Now there would be a real confidence builder for a kid of sixteen."

That night Colt set a watch on Peggy Fowler. She didn't go out, and no one came to their quarters. A watch on Erin Lasser showed that she had two male visitors an hour apart. Both left looking pleased with themselves. Her husband was not seen until he came home from a drinking bout in another enlisted couple's quarters.

Chapter Eleven

The next morning Colt and his four men questioned three more of the "better suspects" in the killings. All were a bit hard in manner and speech. Two of the three admitted having been prostitutes before they got married. The third said she had always wanted to be a dance hall girl, just never had the chance.

All seemed tremendously common, easy going, resigned to their place in life and on this post.

One said it best for all three. "I was a whore plain and simple before I got meself married. Now I'm a wife and mother and I can do the whoring now and then, or whenever I want to — or whenever we're short of cash. Hell, for me and my man, it's a good arrangement."

They let the third one out the front door and Colonel Harding slammed his pad of paper down on the table.

"If this is going to be the pattern, is there any use of talking with the rest of them?"

"The matter of odds, sir," Sergeant Flint

said. "There must be one of them who's a little off center somehow. We're bound to find her if we go through the list."

Colt broke his pencil in half and threw the pieces at the small stove. "Yes, damnit, I know you're right. But let's take the rest of the day off. Don't do anything on the case. Go for a ride in the snow, build a snowman, have a snow fight. But stay away from relaxing with one of our whores. They're all off limits to the four of you until this thing is settled."

"What if we come up with a brilliant idea?" Lieutenant Stanford asked.

"Re-think it, refine it, pare and shape and perfect it. Then tell all of us tomorrow at 9 A.M. right here. We'll decide who to talk to then."

He sent them all out and closed up the office. He was going to spend the afternoon playing with Dan and Sadie. Halfway home through the foot of snow that was left he remembered the birthday party tonight.

This afternoon he was sure he'd be pressed into service to get something ready for the party.

Colt's noon meal was a sandwich and coffee he fixed himself.

"I found five other teens and they're all coming. Including Cynthia Patterson who likes Kirk. She's coming at four to help me

186

finish getting ready and she'll stay for the party."

"Good. Doc Wilshire is having a small poker party tonight. . . ."

"Not on your life, soldier!" Doris's voice cracked like a Top Sergeant, and they both laughed. "I need you here as a chaperon. We're having three young ladies, thirteen to fifteen, and four small gentlemen from thirteen to sixteen. You are restricted to quarters tonight."

"If only this woman understood military jargon. . . ." Colt ducked a pillow Doris threw and then grabbed her for a hug.

The party began as a disaster. The three boys sat on one side of the room and the three girls on the other. They had played Tic Tac Toe, boys against the girls, and the girls won. They had played Pin the Tail on the Donkey, and the girls' team won.

"Have you ever played broom over?" Doris asked. The girls shook their heads. The boys each said a soft no.

"That includes me," Colt said. Doris explained the game. "I'll be in the circle with the broom. My husband will go out of the room and I'll hold the broom over someone and say, 'Broom over.' The Colonel will repeat my words. But when I say, 'Broom over who?' he'll describe the person or give the name of the person I'm holding the broom over. It's really magic. You have to figure out how we do it."

Doris took Colt into the kitchen.

"How?" he said.

"When you're still in the room and we're talking, I'll be leaning on the broom and it will be pointing at the person who is the broom over person. You read the name off the name tag, and when I say broom over who, you'll know who it is. Simple."

They did it three times and the kids couldn't figure it out. Then Doris made it more obvious and Kirk said he knew the secret and wanted to go out of the room. Colt replaced him in the circle.

Kirk got the broom over right the first time.

"I don't see how you did that," Cynthia said.

Kirk grinned. "I'm magical. I know all sorts of things."

They played it twice more and this time Cynthia figured it out.

After that things warmed up a little. They played Winkem, a game where the girls sat in chairs and the boys were behind them. The idea was there was one empty chair and the boy with the empty chair had to wink at one of the girls and she tried to escape to his chair without the boy touching her shoulders.

That loosened things up more and when the ten-thirty time came for dessert, they were more than ready and all knew everyone else. Kirk had been paying a lot of attention to Cynthia.

Sadie and Daniel had been watching the party through a crack where their bedroom door was open.

After apple cobbler dessert, Colt walked all of the kids home. Cynthia was next to last. Colt had noticed that Kirk had been beside her since the dessert time. Kirk waited until Cynthia was safely in her house, then he ran back to Colt.

"Who is that girl?" Colt asked.

"Cynthia, Cynthia Patterson. Her dad's a Captain in infantry, C Company Commander."

"Oh."

"They've only been on the post for three or four months, and I've never met her before."

"Until now."

"Yeah. We're both working on study courses. I'm going over to her house tomorrow to study geography."

Colt waved as Kirk ran up to his front door and vanished inside.

"One small problem settled, I'd wager," Colt said as he walked through the snow back to his quarters.

When Colt got home, Sadie and Dan were at the kitchen table eating up the last of the apple cobbler.

"Hey, save some for me," Colt called.

The next morning at nine, Colt and his crew looked over the names of the remaining prostitutes to interview. Colt was beyond frustration. He assigned the last of the interviewing to Lieutenant Stanford, took a mount from the paddock and had it saddled. He rode around the outside of the fort for two hours hoping the chill of the winter day and the plodding of the horse would stir some new idea in his mind.

When he came back he sat in on the interviewing, speeded it up and made sure the last of the enlisted whores were all talked to that day.

A dispatch rider came through from General Sheridan. In the pouch there was a letter for Colt. Sheridan had moved his field headquarters to Fort Cobb. It was the first day of the new year when Sheridan wrote the message to Colt.

"Moving the base of Indian reserve from Fort Cobb thirty miles south to a new base just being built I'm calling Fort Sill. There is more grass for the horses, more dry land for the Indians. Let me know when you can rejoin me."

Colt threw his pencil against the far wall.

He wanted to be with the troops, with the action. Instead, he was penned up here trying to play detective. He had told them he wasn't a detective. He should just give up and turn the case over to Colonel Erhard and forget about it. Then he could go down to Fort Sill and be a soldier again.

Colt found the pencil, sharpened it with his pocket knife and held his hands over the hot stove. Then he went to his desk and began writing.

"Drastic Measures needed.

"1. Register every whore with the fort medical officer.

"2. Require medical examinations of all whores every month.

"3. Restrict any who do not pass the medical from whoring.

"4. Whores to keep accurate records of each man serviced by date and time.

"5. Any violation of these orders by the whore will result in the woman being shipped to Omaha within a week. Her husband will remain here."

"6. Army enlisted men who act as pimps for their wives must register with the Commanding Officer. Any pimp not registering will be cashiered from the service immediately.

"7. No new whores will be registered for

this camp. Any woman operating as a prostitute for money who is not registered will be summarily shipped out to Omaha on the next wagon train.

"8. Any enlisted man who willingly lets his wife violate any of these orders, will be cashiered from the service immediately."

Colt read the orders again, made a few word changes and carried them over to Colonel Erhard's office. The Fort Commander welcomed him into his office.

"Any results?" Erhard asked.

"Damn few, if any. A suggestion. I want these orders issued from your office. We start turning screws down on the whores and the pimps until one of them cracks and we have our killer."

The Fort Commander read the eight orders.

"A little tough on the fancy ladies, don't you think?"

"I don't care. It's tougher on the three men somebody murdered. We put them all on the rack and start stretching them and somebody is going to give up or make a big mistake. Either way we have our killer."

Colonel Erhard stared at the paper, then called in his clerk. He signed the paper Colt had written.

"Put this order out to be read at all company formations and posted on the company announcement board. As of last call today."

The clerk nodded and left.

"Phil moved his base of operations again, I see," Colonel Erhard said.

"Don't remind me. That's where I should be right now instead of trying to be a damn Pinkerton."

"You'll have plenty of Indians to fight. The experts say we've got at least ten more years of Indian wars." He stabbed a look at Colt. "What happens if this notice doesn't produce some results?"

"Then we really get tough. I'll have to figure out what to do next. Maybe threaten to ship all the whores out of camp unless we find the killer. Somebody might know something they aren't saying about one of their own."

"Possible." Colonel Erhard lit a cigar. He blew a ring of smoke that caved in. "Hear you damn near panicked an infantry company yesterday riding off-saddle, Indian style."

"Friend and I put on a little demonstration."

"You'll have to show me sometime."

"I will, after I get back from Fort Sill." Colt left and stormed back to his small office where the interviewing continued. Sergeant Flint said they had found nothing out of the ordinary yet. They had three more to go.

It would not produce a suspect, Colt knew. What the hell next?

Watchers. He'd put his three enlisted on night watch on three of the women. But which three? His one candidate was Peggy Fowler. Who else? He'd get the other two from Sergeant Flint. This time it had to work. If it didn't he was going to be the one they locked up in the crazy house!

Chapter Twelve

The next morning in his small office, Colt stood beside the fire Sergeant Flint had started and let the warmth soak into his bones. Some of these crisp clear mornings he didn't think he'd ever be warm again.

Sergeant Flint knocked on the door and opened it.

"Beg your pardon Colonel, but there's a lady here to see you. She said it's extremely important."

Colt lifted his brows. It might be good news. He hoped. "Have her come in."

She stepped into the room and nodded.

"Good morning, I'm Colonel Harding."

The woman stood there a moment, then nodded. She seemed so nervous that she couldn't speak.

"Sergeant Flint, could we have two cups of coffee please. And some of those cinnamon rolls."

Colt looked at the woman. "Now, please, come over by the fire and get warmed up. Nothing like a good freezing Kansas winter to make you appreciate a humid, boiling hot Kansas summer."

The woman smiled and nodded.

Colt held out his hand. "My name is Colt Harding," he said.

"Oh, I'm Harriet Jergens."

Sergeant Flint brought in a tray with three cinnamon rolls on it and two cups of coffee. Colt handed one to Mrs. Jergens and took one himself.

When she had sampled the coffee and nibbled at a roll, Colt tried to get things moving.

"Sergeant Flint said you had something to tell me, Mrs. Jergens. I want you to relax and not be uneasy. This is just an office like any other one. You're married to one of our enlisted men here on the post?"

"Yes, sir."

"And you've never talked to a colonel before. I bet that's why you're so nervous?"

She smiled and nodded. "Yes, sir. Scared stiff. I hear so much from my husband about officers . . . and all . . ."

"Right now, Mrs. Jergens, I don't feel much like an army officer. I'm more of a Pinkerton detective. I've never met one but they say they are just ordinary men, a lot of them former policemen and sheriffs and marshals. Now, what do you have that you need to tell me?"

196

"Colonel, I'm a laundry and cleaning woman but I'm not a prostitute. I'd never do that. If some of the laundry women want to, fine, but not me. I was cleaning that day that the officer was murdered. It was the same day, and I was doing Captain Wilson's rooms. He's unmarried. I was ready to come out of his rooms after I finished and I saw somebody coming out of quarters down the way.

"I'd opened the door but hadn't stepped out yet. I remembered it was strange because those quarters was empty. They belonged to that officer who was killed at Washita. Then I decided they must have put a new officer in there. I saw her close the door and walk toward the laundry room. It was in the afternoon about three, 'cause that's when I get through with the Wilson quarters."

"You're sure it was the same day the officer was murdered?" Colt asked evenly.

"Yes, sir."

"You're sure it was his quarters that you saw the woman come out of."

"Yes, I'm positive."

Colt walked to the window and came back. He looked down at the woman who sat beside the stove.

"This is tremendously important, Mrs. Jergens. Think carefully before you answer. Can you identify — without any doubt — the woman who came out of the dead officer's quarters?"

"Yes sir, absolutely."

"Who was she, Mrs. Jergens?"

"I'd know her anywhere. She has a washtub right beside mine and she teases me because I'm not a whore. I tease her right back and we get on fine. Her name is Peggy Fowler."

"How do you know it was the day the officer was killed?"

"Because I always do the Wilson rooms on Thursday. That was the day the officer was murdered."

"How far away were you from the woman coming from the dead officer's room?"

"Two quarters down, maybe thirty, forty feet."

"At that distance you recognized Peggy Fowler with no chance of a mistake?"

"Yes, sir. No chance at all. Known her for three years."

"Mrs. Jergens, why didn't you come forward with this information before?"

"Wasn't sure it was so important. The man could have been killed after Peggy left. Didn't want to get her in trouble."

"And now?"

"Nobody else charged with his killing. I figured there was a chance it could be Peggy or she might know something about it, so I better tell you." She paused and her hand trembled as she set the coffee cup down. "I . . . I won't get my husband in any trouble, will I? He just got his Corporal stripes and he'd yell at me if I hurt his career."

Colt chuckled. "Not at all, Mrs. Jergens. It could even help. I was talking a little stern with you just now because that's how some officer will talk to you at the court martial if Peggy is charged with the killing."

"I understand. I seen a court martial once."

"Mrs. Jergens, will you write out what you just told me and then sign it? We'll need the record to start any proceedings we might launch against Peggy Fowler."

"Oh, yes. I can write. Yes."

When she left ten minutes later, Colt smiled broadly. He called in Sergeant Flint and the others who had arrived and said they might have a break.

"Any action by Peggy Fowler last night?"

One of the Privates yawned. "Excuse me, sir. No action, but her light was on in the Fowler quarters until past midnight, but nobody came or went."

He told them about Mrs. Jergens's statement. They cheered.

"Not a word about this goes outside this room. Now we really start watching Peggy

Fowler! We put somebody on her day and night!"

Trooper Mel Fowler stared at the orders posted on the notice board in his company orderly room. Damn, but they were getting snotty about this. What business of theirs was it about the whoring on post. Fucking officers!

He had to register? Where the hell did he register as a pimp? Damn, they were getting downright nasty! He'd ask a couple of the guys he knew who set up their wives. They should know. Christ, all of this and Peggy acting spooky. She screamed like a stuck pig the other day when he said he had a two dollar lay lined up for her. How did he know she had the rag on again?

Mel knew this whole damn hoorah of special orders and interviews and medical examinations for the women was over them three guys who got themselves murdered. They must think a whore did it. The way their prick and balls were slashed up, it figured. What the hell, it couldn't be a whore, why would one want to cut up a paying customer?

He had made damn sure that the three murder victims were not men he had set up with Peggy. She never came near them. That was fine to know since he had to go to sleep beside Peggy every night.

Still something bothered him. Peggy had been out the night that second enlisted man died. Said she was at a cleaning woman friend's house. He'd never checked.

He snorted and walked outside. What the hell. Was he trying to talk himself into the idea that his own damn wife had killed them three men? Was he?

Jesus . . . it was possible. She could get goddamn mad sometimes. That one time she was liquored up she came at him with a knife. He didn't even know she had it. Carried it in a little sheath on her ankle all covered up by them long skirts.

The doubts kept lingering as he finished his duty and went home. Melvin watched Peggy that evening as she fixed their supper. Was she nervous? Was she normal? Hell, he couldn't tell. When she had the dishes done she combed her hair and put on a heavy coat.

"I'm going to visit a friend. It's Milly, she done got herself a bad case of the cold and we don't want no pneumonia. Be back in a couple of hours."

Mel growled and went back to warming his hands over the little heating stove. Two hours? Time enough for her to service four guys someplace. Had she been stepping out on him like this and taking the cash herself?

The little bitch! He'd follow her and catch her in the damn act!

Peggy left about eight. Melvin was close behind her, but staying in the shadows, trailing her craftily. She never looked behind her. She was so damn confident she had him fooled! Melvin growled to himself as he watched her.

She went to the stables, slipped past the guard who wasn't paying attention, and then opened the tack room where the saddles and harness and all the cavalry gear was stored.

So that was where she worked for herself, Melvin fumed. She probably paid off the guard to let her use the bunk back there. It took him five minutes to get around the guard, then he moved to the tack room and eased open the door.

He got it closed without a sound and he stopped and listened. At first he heard nothing, then from down toward the Sergeant's room he heard a soft moan of desire. It was Peggy. She was faking it for some bastard on top of her!

Mel pulled the revolver from his belt, cocked it and moved on silent feet toward the room halfway down the long building. When he got to the door it was open a crack. There was no light in the room. A lantern left burning in the tack room gave an eerie light. It seemed dark inside the smaller room.

"Oh, yes! Harder, harder!" a voice said from inside.

It was Peggy. He knew that voice. She was putting on her phoney excited voice to urge the customer on. Melvin wondered how many she had whored this way without telling him. What did she do with the money?

Damn, but he was gonna have one sweet time slapping her ass around! He'd beat up the damn customer first, then take care of Peggy. It was gonna be one sweet time!

Melvin Fowler pushed the door open and stepped into the dark room as he scratched a match on the wall.

"What the hell's going on in here?" he bellowed.

Just as the match flared he saw something to his left, then whatever it was hit him on the side of the head and he went down on the tack room office floor as wave after wave of pain and blackness threatened him. He pushed up to a sitting position, then something hit his head again and he went down and into total blackness.

When Melvin came back to reality, he felt a gigantic sledge hammer smashing around inside his head.

"Oh god! What hit me?"

He blinked and saw that it was light in the room. Yes, it was the Sergeant's room and two lamps burned brightly.

"What the hell is going on?" Mel asked. Then he tried to move. He couldn't. His hands and feet were tied to the Sergeant's bunk. He sensed someone in back of his head where he couldn't see them.

"Come on out, you bastard!" Melvin roared.

"Why not, you're awake now and can enjoy it, enjoy the whole thing." Peggy came around where he could see her. She was fully clothed and held a thin knife in her hand. The blade was four inches long and looked razor sharp.

"Peggy! What the hell?"

"About right. Hell is where we're both going. But you get to go first. Only sorry about one thing, Mel. I had the mistake of doing in them three men, carving them up fine. All the time I should have let them be and sunk my blade into you." She slashed with the knife and cut open his shirt. In the process she cut a thin blood line down his chest.

"Oh, was that a little deep, sorry." From the shirt pieces she tore out a long strip and tied it around his head and through his yelling mouth, gagging him. His voice was throttled to a whimper.

She hummed to herself as she worked now, using the knife to cut all of his clothes off him. When he was naked she lifted his limp penis

204

with the dull side of the knife.

"Well, well, well, look at the little prick we found here. Just be patient little guy, your turn is coming."

She sliced a deep cut down Melvin's cheek. He screamed in pain and rage.

"I knew you'd follow me tonight, Melvin. I gave you enough clues not to trust me. You finally caught on. You're stupid, Melvin, know that? Damn stupid.

"I married you to get out of whoring, and six months later you had me flipping on my back again. Only this time you made the money. You bastard!"

She sliced him again this time on his chest. Melvin blubbered in pain.

"Hey, Melvin. No rush. I've been whoring for you for what, four or five years now? All I'm asking of you is just this one night. You can give that much. You owe me!"

Peggy lifted the blade and shook her head at Melvin, then drove the knife downward. It stabbed through the black hairs on his belly, driving in to the hilt.

Melvin jolted upward as far as he could go, then he babbled and cried through the gag. They had been words but now they made no sense.

Peggy shook the blade once, then drew it out straight and Melvin passed out. She got a wet towel from a bucket of water and sloshed cold water over his face.

"Wake up, Melvin. We can't have our little party without you being awake."

Trooper Melvin Fowler shivered and shook his head. The pain engulfed him and he almost passed out again. He looked at Peggy, his face twisted into hatred. But no words could get through the gag.

Peggy smiled. "Well, now, the star of our show is here, we can get on with the entertainment."

Outside the stables, Sergeant Flint talked with the regular interior guard. He'd been on duty for two hours and was sure that no one had gone into the stables or the tack room area.

Sergeant Flint shook his head in disgust. "Private, if this were Comanche country, you'd be dead by now. A woman and a man both slipped past you when you were at the far end of your post. They're in there right now. I'm following the woman. I just saw her come out of her house, then her own husband slips out and starts following her. Now I have two people to tail."

"What the hell they doing in there?"

"Not the slightest idea. She might have been meeting somebody for whoring. I don't know. If they don't come out in an hour, I'm going to call my Colonel. I'd say your ass is in a big lot of trouble right now for not challenging those two people when they went past you."

Back inside the tack room, Peggy took a spur from a hook. She lay the metal over the chimney of one of the lamps, balancing it against the wall so it would stay in place.

She had been busy with the knife. Long slices showed down Melvin Fowler's chest and sides. His arms were totally covered with blood from slashes.

Peggy made sure Melvin was still conscious, then she checked the spur over the lamp chimney. Yes, hot enough.

She took the spur and holding it by the leather fasteners, brought the red hot rowel down firmly on Melvin's chest. There was a short sizzle as the metal burned into flesh, and a wisp of smoke, then she pulled the spur away. A good brand, the rowel burned into the skin to leave the mark.

She put the spur down and took her knife again. It was still sharp. The knife descended on his genitals. She smiled as the blade drove into him. Melvin gave a muffled scream and passed out. Peggy shook her head. The man had no staying power. The very first slice through a testicle and he fainted again. She watched the blood ooze out of the orb. It looked different every time she cut one.

Now she went to work in earnest. She sliced and pruned and cut and cut off and when she was satisfied, leaned back and checked her work on Melvin's crotch.

"Yes, it passes inspection." She listened to his breathing. Shallow and irregular. Her finger at his neck told her that his pulse was weak and fast, as if his heart was speeding up to get enough blood to his body. All it did was pump more red out of the hundred cuts on his body.

She tried the cold water in his face. It washed away the blood but didn't wake him. Poor Melvin was so tired he might never wake up again. She'd been too long already. She didn't want anyone to find her like this. Far, far better the other way.

"Goodbye, Melvin," she said. A tear eased out of her eye and rolled down her cheek. "There were some good times, but too many bad times. If I wanted to be a whore, I could have stayed with Ida. At least she gave me a day off now and then, and I always had nice dresses and even bonnets. I still don't know what you did with the money. I made more than you did every month. So you took it."

She lifted the knife and placed it over Melvin's neck on the left side. She slashed it suddenly slicing open the carotid artery.

Blood surged six feet into the room in a

long spurt. Part of it hit her in the chest. The spurts came two a second for a while. Then the pressure eased, the blood surge slowed and then suddenly the blood stopped.

She knew he was dead. She took both knives and stabbed them in Melvin's heart, then shook her head and slipped out the door to the Sergeant's quarters. She left the lamps on. Melvin shouldn't have to wait in the dark.

Peggy moved slowly the way out that she had decided. She left her heavy coat in the Sergeant's room. She walked to the far end of the tack room and found the other outside door which was locked and barred from the inside. Peggy lifted out the heavy wooden bar, then unlocked the door and edged it open just enough so she could slip through.

No one challenged her. Once outside, she pushed the door closed again. She was on the far end of the stable complex. To her right lay the fence that enclosed the paddock. To the far left were the cavalry barracks. Straight ahead lay only the Kansas plains and a half foot of snow. She could probably walk for 20 miles and not see a living soul.

Peggy began to walk forward. It was cold. Must be well below zero. At first she pulled her thin dress around her. Then she let it hang. It didn't matter. Five minutes later she was well away from the fort. She looked back once, shrugged and kept going. She blew on her hands. Her fingers were cold, maybe frost bitten by now. Her feet felt like chunks of ice.

Peggy wore only her thin dress and under things.

That was the way she had planned it, too. It was time. She was tired. Life had been almost twenty-six years. Hell, that was long enough for any whore.

She walked another half mile, then stumbled and fell. She got up and kept walking. The third time she fell, Peggy Fowler couldn't rise. She lay there in the crusty snow. She reached under the crust to get some of the softer snow and pushed it into her mouth with frozen fingers.

Yes, it tasted good. Pure, cold.

She had heard that it was easy. You just sat down in the snow and went to sleep. She wasn't sleepy. Maybe she should walk farther. Peggy looked at the dim lights of the fort. She must be two or three miles away. Far enough.

She blinked and felt the drowsiness creeping over her. There was a tingling in her thighs now, but no feeling at all in her hands or feet. Even her breasts tingled with the chill. She looked up at the stars. They were out bright tonight.

Stars! Maybe she would go live on a star. Maybe. They must be far away. How long would it take her to get there?

Peggy thought about Melvin for just a moment. He got what he deserved, sweet justice. After all these years! Peggy laughed but no sound came out. She tried to open her mouth, but realized her lips must be frozen together.

They didn't hurt. Her fingers and toes and feet didn't hurt. Sleepy. Yes, she was really getting sleepy now. Tired. Life had been so hard. Sleepy.

Peggy closed her eyes and went to sleep.

Chapter Thirteen

Sergeant Flint stomped his feet and swung his arms as he stood near the guard outside the stables. He wished he could find a thermometer. It had to be well below zero. He pulled a pocket watch out at last and struck a match to look at the time.

"Damn! They've been in there almost two hours now." He hit the guard on the shoulder. "I want you to call for the Corporal of the Guard."

The guard looked at Flint. "I ain't never done that before. They said not to do that unless something was damned bad."

Sergeant Flint ignored the man. "Corporal of the Guard!" he bellowed. "Corporal of the Guard!" He looked at the surprised trooper. "What post is this?"

"Four."

"Corporal of the Guard, post number four!"

Sergeant Flint stopped then and heard his call repeated down the line. Four minutes later by Flint's watch the Sergeant of the

212

Guard ran up with his Spencer rifle at port arms.

Sergeant Flint took over. "Guard Sergeant, I'm working with Colonel Harding. He should be called to this point immediately. Check his quarters first. On the double, Sergeant!"

The Sergeant looked at him, remembered the name of Colonel Harding and ran back toward the guard house and the officer quarters.

Nearly eight minutes later Colt ran up to Sergeant Flint. He gave Colt a brief report of what had happened so far.

"Far as I know, both of them are still inside. There are other exits, but they aren't used much."

Colt grabbed a lantern from the stables, lit it and carried it into the tack room. He stopped just inside the door. All was quiet. Colt moved forward, the lantern in his left hand, one of the twin pearl handled revolvers in his right.

"There's a light on down there," Flint said. "Looks like the tack Sergeant's office."

The door stood half open as they approached it. Still there was no sound.

Colt saw two lamps burning in the small room. He stood beside the door and pushed it fully open with his foot.

"My god!" Colt spat. "Go get Doctor Wilshire, Flint."

The trooper saw the body lying on the cot, saw the blood.

"Another one!" he said as he spun around and ran for the medical officer.

A half hour later Dr. Wilshire, Colt and Colonel Erhard agreed, it was another killing by the same person.

"This time we know who it is," Colt said. "She at last vented all of her anger on the person who deserved it, her husband. Peggy Fowler is the person who killed all four of those men. Now all we have to do is find her."

As soon as he told Doctor Wilshire to report to the stables, Sergeant Flint had gone to the Fowler quarters. The lights were off and no one answered the door. He called the Sergeant of the Guard who opened the unlocked door and inspected the quarters. Mrs. Fowler was not there.

Flint told Colt.

"You said there were other exits out of this part of the stables," Colt said. "Show me." Sergeant Flint took him to one exit through the haymow. It was locked and bolted from inside. It led out to a ten foot drop off where hay wagons could unload.

"The only other one is down here," Sergeant Flint said.

214

They found the door at the far end of the stables. It was unlocked and unbolted.

Colt called for the lantern and pushed open the door. He checked the virgin snow in the area and quickly found the footprints of one person walking straight away from the fort.

"I'll follow them," Colt barked. "Flint, go saddle two horses and ride west following these tracks. You can see them in the moonlight. Let's move, now!"

Colt jogged forward through the snow. He sunk up to his ankles through the crust with each step and his running soon turned into a fast walk. He took long strides to cut down the time of getting in and out of the crust.

He walked for what he figured was half a mile before he heard the horses coming. Colt mounted one of the animals and they continued the tracking, cantering along at a brisk pace, then checking the prints and moving out faster again.

They were out over a mile and a half when they found a place a person had fallen.

Colt examined the area. He saw nothing but the mashed down snow.

"Small footprints, sir," Flint said.

"Yes, it's a woman all right, and probably Peggy. Did you see that heavy woman's coat in the death room? It was there, carefully folded over a chair. This has all the signs of a

215

woman who is trying to let herself be frozen to death."

They rode again. Twice more they found where she had fallen, then ahead in the snow they saw a dark form.

Both men spurred their mounts ahead. Colt leaped off his animal and knelt in the snow.

Peggy Fowler lay on her side in the snow, her head nestled on her arm. Blood showed on the sleeve and front of her dress. There was a soft smile on her face even in repose. She wasn't breathing. Colt felt her throat for a pulse but could find none.

"She's dead. No coat, no gloves, no boots. She walked until she couldn't move any further. Then she must have simply gone to sleep and been dead in ten minutes."

Her body wasn't quite frozen stiff. They picked her up and tied her on one of the horses, then both men walked their mounts back to the fort. There was no hurry now.

The next morning Colt, Colonel Erhard and Doctor Captain Wilshire gathered in the Fort Commander's office. The four reports of the four murders lay on the Commander's table.

They had talked over the facts as they knew them in the case of Trooper Melvin Fowler. There was only one conclusion that they could draw.

"We all agree then, that the death of Melvin Fowler was at the hand of his wife, done by knife?"

The other men both said a firm yes.

"And Dr. Wilshire, do you state that each of these four deaths was perpetrated in almost identical fashion, using the same strokes of the knife on the same parts of the body, the same ritual, and the final death blow by cutting the neck artery?"

"Yes, sir, I do."

"Then it's the decision of this council that all four deaths were carried out by the same person, namely Mrs. Peggy Fowler, and that all four cases shall be closed and the appropriate reports be forwarded to Department headquarters for processing."

Colonel Erhard looked at Colt. "In the matter of the death of a civilian, Mrs. Peggy Fowler, do you Colonel Harding find that her death came by her own will if not at her own hand. That she did, evidently on purpose, leave the stables by the back door and walk due west into the snow away from all areas of the fort, and away from all habitation."

"I so find."

"And with those stipulations, do you have an opinion on the death of Mrs. Peggy Fowler?"

"I do," Colt said. "It's my opinion that after

inflicting as much pain as possible on her husband and then killing him, she walked into the snow in a suicide act, knowing that she could not go far dressed as lightly as she was. She knew the winters, knew how cold it was, and she had left her coat behind in the tack room office."

The colonel's clerk scrambled to write down word for word what Colt had said. The rest of it had been prepared in advance in writing. The officers all signed the reports.

"That's done with," Colonel Erhard said. "Now we can get on with the business of fighting Indians."

"Which means I'll be moving out shortly to join General Sheridan. He must be at Fort Sill by now. Did he order any supplies or ammunition brought down to him?"

Colonel Erhard built ridges in his brow a moment. "No, he said he was getting everything he needed from Camp Supply. He did ask for another troop of cavalry from the post."

"Can they be ready to ride in three days?" Colt asked.

"If they can't, I'll turn them into infantry."

"Good. I'll have the orders cut. I'll also release my four men to the First Sergeant. Between now and then I plan on being with the family."

Colt nodded to the Colonel and the doctor, then went outside and across the six inches of crusty snow toward the Troop J orderly room he had been using as an office.

He was halfway across when a screeching yell stopped him short. He looked behind him to see a cavalry horse riding directly at him at gallop. All of the rider he saw was a toe locked firmly in the left stirrup and the brown haired head of a youth looking out from under the horse's neck.

"Bang, bang!" the young voice shouted as Kirk Rossman charged past. He lifted into the saddle and walked the mount back to Colt.

"That's a fine move, Trooper. You should be ready to train your father's riders."

A grin spread over Kirk's face in an instant. "Thanks. My father says I can't train his men but I can give a demonstration. Then I'll teach one Sergeant and he'll train the men. But I can watch."

"That sounds great. Keep up those studies if you want to go to West Point. Where are you headed?"

"Oh, I'm going over to see Cynthia Patterson, Captain Patterson's daughter. She was at my birthday party. We're working on math and geography. She's good on geography and I'm teaching her algebra and geometry."

"Sounds like a good trade. Don't be late."

Kirk grinned and rode on across the parade ground doing the off saddle move once more to startle a pair of officers.

Colt continued to his temporary offices. The three enlisted men and Lieutenant Stanford jumped to attention.

"As you were, men." He watched them. "This is the end of the assignment. As of right now you're back in the army, no more soft duty. Report back to your regular duty assignments."

He paused and looked at each man, then went up and called him by name and shook his hand.

"Thanks for helping on this one. Now we move on."

The men snapped to attention, saluted, and Colt walked out the door.

A few minutes later, Colt pushed open the door to his quarters and found Doris up to her elbows in cake batter. Colt walked up behind her and kissed her behind the ear. She dropped her pans and turned in his arms.

"Soldier, you do that once more and I'll tear off my clothes and make passionate love to you here on the kitchen table."

She had whispered it. They both laughed. Danny and Sadie came in and they both grabbed Colt's hands, pulling him into the dining room.

"We're playing war with the dominoes and Danny wants to be the General all the time," Sadie whined.

"So let him be the General. You be the Colonel, because we know that the Colonels do all the work."

The two went behind their "front lines" and snapped dominoes across a two foot no-man's land at the other's fort which was also built of dominoes. It was a good thing Colt had bought double nines.

He watched them for a minute and went back to the kitchen.

"How long before you leave for Fort Sill?" Doris asked.

"Three days. How did you know I'd be going?"

"Oh damn!" She lifted her brows. "I know, it's your job, it's your life, it's the food in our mouths. I just knew you'd go if you could. I surrender."

He sat in the kitchen watching her and soon the cake was in the primitive oven in the brand new kitchen range. The heat was uneven and it usually baked more on one side of the pan than the other unless you turned the pan around halfway through the bake cycle.

"She killed all of them, didn't she?" Doris said.

"Yes, positively. Nobody else could have

copied her technique. And we didn't find any other suspects. If she hadn't butchered her husband for just cause, we never would have caught her."

"Did knowing her and talking to her help?" Doris asked.

"Help how?"

"Help you understand how women think."

Colt snorted, then he laughed. "Help? Not a chance. It put me back about five years in what I thought I already understood about you wiley creatures. I should be a sailor, I'm totally at sea when it comes to the female mind."

"Good," Doris said. "We want to keep it that way. It makes it easier for us because we women understand precisely how men think."

"You don't."

"We do. You're going to get back down there with General Sheridan hoping that he'll give you a command of a regiment of cavalry or maybe two, so you can strike for your permanent rank of Bird Colonel before the Indian fighting is over."

"Glory, the woman has it on the nose."

Much later that night as they lay in bed in the soft afterglow of delicious lovemaking, Doris leaned up on one elbow and stared at him.

"Do you really hope that Sheridan gives

you a cavalry regiment?"

"My wife said it, she's never wrong."

Doris punched him in the chest. Colt caught her and held her.

But already he was thinking about strategy and moves. There were still a lot of Cheyenne and Arapaho west of the Wichita Mountains. Black Kettle's sister was at the reserve. They might be able to use her some way as an emissary. Then there was Little Raven still outside with his Arapaho.

Colt grinned as he lay there with Doris. In another four days he'd be on his way back to the action.

Back to the Indian Wars!

The employees of Thorndike Press hope you have enjoyed this Large Print book. All our Large Print titles are designed for easy reading, and all our books are made to last. Other Thorndike Press Large Print books are available at your library, through selected bookstores, or directly from the publishers.

For more information about titles, please call:

(800) 223-1244
(800) 223-6121

To share your comments, please write:

Publisher
Thorndike Press
295 Kennedy Memorial Drive
Waterville, ME 04901

X   3/04   4   1/04
    1/07   12   1/07
    5/08   15   3/08
    1/15   (26)   7/13